MISS ADVENTURE #2

Beauty Queen BLOWOUT

LILLA AND NORA ZUCKERMAN

A FIRESIDE BOOK
PUBLISHED BY SIMON & SCHUSTER
NEW YORK LONDON TORONTO SYDNEY SINGAPORE

FIRESIDE
Rockefeller Center
1230 Avenue of the Americas
New York, NY 10020

Copyright © 2003 by Lilla and Nora Zuckerman
All rights reserved,
including the right of reproduction
in whole or in part in any form.

FIRESIDE and colophon are registered trademarks of Simon & Schuster Inc.

Designed by Michelle Blau

For information about special discounts for bulk purchases,
please contact Simon & Schuster Special Sales:
1-800-456-6798 or business@simonandschuster.com

Manufactured in the United States of America

1   3   5   7   9   10   8   6   4   2

Library of Congress Cataloging-in-Publication Data

Zuckerman, Lilla.
Beauty queen blowout / Lilla and Nora Zuckerman.
p.   cm.
1. Beauty contests—Fiction. I. Zuckerman, Nora. II. Title III. Series.
PS3626.U27B43 2003
813'.6—dc21
2003045489
ISBN 0-7432-3846-X

Stop right there! Read this first!

This is a *Miss Adventure*! Meaning, this book is interactive—not one of those stodgy old books where you start reading on the first page and finish on the last. At the end of every chapter you will be asked to make a decision and flip to the corresponding page. You're in the driver's seat, so think carefully—your decisions may make the difference between becoming a Miss Liberty beauty queen, or becoming a trashy tabloid scandal queen.

This is your *Miss Adventure,* so have a ball—and **no cheating!** True Miss Adventurers accept their fate with grace and poise. Smile that perfect smile and wave like a princess because in this *Miss Adventure,* the swimsuit competition makes up 20 percent of your final score!

MISS ADVENTURE #2

Beauty Queen
BLOWOUT

One week of dance rehearsal, three days of preliminary interviews, months of preparations, and all because your friends dared you to enter a regional beauty pageant one year ago. Amazingly you are now Miss Vermont, the dark horse contender to become Miss Liberty, the winner of America's most beloved and prestigious beauty pageant. The live television broadcast is tomorrow, when the whole country and every kid you ever went to school with will either be rooting for or against you.

To say things snowballed would be an understatement. You never really paid much attention to this pageant stuff; you may have even denounced it as shallow at one point. Your coworkers back home always said you had a Miss Liberty smile, but it was just a running joke. Then they dared you to enter the Miss Liberty Burlington pageant as a prank, and you only said yes because entering meant you would get a case of the beer of your choice from each of them. Needless to say they were floored when you won, but no one was more shocked than you were by the whopping check that came with winning the regional title.

Now here you are in Reno, Nevada, "The Biggest Little City in the World," smack dab in the middle of pageant head-quarters in the famous Aces Casino Towers. As you walk across the world's ugliest carpet toward the hotel elevators, you realize how much your feet are killing you and how painful it is to smile all day long, but there's no way you're giving up now. Surprisingly, you have come to really want to win this thing: Be it a ping-pong game or a beauty pageant, you always want to come out the victor. As expected, so do all the other fifty-one girls in the pageant. Hell, your chances aren't even one in fifty; outside of the official states, you're up against Miss District of Columbia and Miss U.S. Territories. All of these girls have been dreaming about this all their lives. You're definitely the rookie of the pageant circuit, and such achievement so quickly is unheard of. These polished pageant veterans think you lucked into this. And they're right.

"Hold the elevator!" you call out, trotting toward the closing doors. The girls inside—both Carolinas and Oklahoma—pretend not to hear you, so the doors close on your face. You only have to wait a minute for the next one to show up, and you're kind of relieved to be alone. You would give your right arm for a deep tissue massage and a stiff martini. It's been one hell of a week.

The judges are a motley crew of old pageant winners who take this way too seriously, a sleazy guy named Réné who doesn't seem serious about anything but the swimsuit competition, one former gymnastics golden girl with a thirteen-year-old body and a thirty-five-year-old face, and a Nobel prize–winner who looks hopelessly lost. The host of the nationally televised pageant is Roddy Topper, a man who's so tanned he probably drinks bronzer for breakfast. America seems to love his talk show, but you can't get past his co-host, Cricket McCall, whose voice has been known to give people seizures. Then there's the pageant director, Fanny Mae Briar, who spends all year grooming "her girls" for this one event, which she feels will instill morality and goodness in America. But her main goal is impressing Daniel Aces, the uber-wealthy sponsor of the pageant. The Miss Liberty pageant takes place in his hotel, his theater, and is paid for with his money, so his name is *everywhere.* The whole pageant is practically an advertisement for his casino empire.

There's a lot at stake for the Miss Liberty contestants, too. Not only is there a huge cash prize (you can kiss those student loans good-bye), but it also means a year of travel, promotions, and charity work. Oh, and there's the prestige. Once you're Miss Liberty, the title sticks with you for a lifetime.

When you get to your room, your keycard is barely in the scanner when you hear, "Vermont!" It's the badass local girl, Miss Nevada. You don't believe the rumors about her—that she used to pole-dance, that she won the state title in a card game, that she already turned down an offer from *Playboy*—you just like her refreshing how-the-hell'd-I-get-here? attitude. She is flanked by Miss Delaware and Miss District of Columbia. You've noticed that for some reason, the little states tend to stick together.

"We're sick of being cooped up in here and we're getting out!" Miss Nevada says. "I know this great roadhouse bar off the beaten path."

"A bar? Isn't that against the rules?" you ask, realizing this may be the first time you've ever asked that question.

"Technically not," she says. "But it's kind of a tradition."

It's been a long week—and you do deserve a little fun time. But swilling alcohol (and let's face it, in your condition you'll drink whatever they're pouring) is not the best thing to do if you've got to compete tomorrow. Do you want to have a noticeable beer bloat during the swimsuit competition? On national television?

You're contemplating this as Miss Montana comes prancing down the hall like the show pony she thinks she is. In truth, she has horrible teeth and knows she can't win so she's been gunning for the Miss Congeniality title from the moment she got here.

"Oh, don't you dare steal her away!" squeals Miss Montana. "You're staying right here tonight—I'm throwing an old-fashioned pajama-jammy-jam down the hall. We snuck some candy bars from the vending machines and Miss Kansas, that little lush, got a bottle of peach schnapps past Fanny Mae! We're just gonna tell funny stories and hang out like old girlfriends!"

Normally, you'd run and hide from Miss Montana, but the pajama party does seem like the smart thing to do. Going out drinking the night before the pageant is kind of a dangerous thing, and you know you'll have the edge over those girls if they wake up with hangovers. Sips of peach schnapps and first-kiss stories might be just the thing you need to decompress. Besides, you really haven't gotten to know Miss Montana's posse yet.

"So Vermont, what'll it be?" says Miss Montana.

If you decide to blow off your beauty sleep and enjoy some local color with Miss Nevada, turn to page 7.

If you can put up with Miss Montana's fake smile for some real girl-bonding, prepare to jammy-jam and turn to page 11.

You have had enough slumber parties to last you a lifetime. A night of "light as a feather, stiff as a board" may put you over the edge.

You turn to Miss Montana apologetically.

"I'm sorry Montana, it's just that the last time I went to a slumber party, I woke up and found my panties in the freezer. It was really traumatic. Hope you understand."

She gives you a sympathetic smile and says, "Totally understand, hon. I once peed my sleeping bag 'cause of that old hot water trick. We'll eat a peanut M&M for you!"

She dashes down the hall to find a new victim.

Miss Nevada grabs your arm and leads you down the hall to the elevators with the other girls. "You're gonna love this place," she says with a grin. "Far enough away from the city but close enough to the action." You decide it's wiser not to ask how she became such an expert on local "action." "No one there will recognize us."

The four of you try to exit the casino without drawing too much attention, but stealth is difficult since you are four statuesque beauties with enormous hair. As you stride through the casino, you collect catcalls and whistles. In the midst of all the midwestern tourists, a handsome and sophisticated-looking young man holding a rack of casino chips walks right toward you. You hold eye contact with him, noticing his perfectly gelled hair, crisp button-down shirt, and very expensive shoes. As he passes you he whispers "Damn." You smile in satisfaction and head through the glass revolving doors.

"Have you heard a word I said?" complains Miss Nevada. Puzzled, you glance at her. "Money?" she whispers. "For the cab? I only have plastic." You hand her a lump of cash from your purse.

A twenty-minute cab ride later, you arrive at a roadside cowboy bar. The parking lot is filled with semis, pickups, and a couple of stray dogs. A flashing neon sign above the entrance to the bar says "Naughty Lil's." And the bar? It's basically an old red barn that now houses kegs instead of live-stock. "Oh my God," Delaware says in horror, "it's straight out of *Porky's*!"

"Try *The Accused*," you say, hoping there's no pinball machine in the back room.

"Come on you princesses. Jesus Christ, one beauty pageant and you've all turned into little pussy cats," Nevada huffs.

She has a point. She pulls you through the door into a cav-ernous bar where the main design motif seems to be thou-sands of bras stapled to the rafters.

"How quaint," District of Columbia sneers to Nevada, "the floors are even covered in sawdust. If this fucks up my pedicure, it's your ass."

"Shut up and get a drink," Nevada orders. That may be the best idea she's had all night. You wiggle up to the bar between a trucker and a kid with a fantastic mullet and a pinkie ring. A haggard barmaid throws down a napkin and takes your order.

"Can you make a Manhattan?" you ask. She gives you a

blank stare. "Vodka gimlet?" Still no recognition in her eyes. "How about a Jack and Coke," you say, resigned. She starts to pour. Just then, you hear a bone-chilling cry behind you.

"Oh my gracious!" a girl's voice shrills, "I cannot believe it!" You whip around to face her. With her helmet of blonde hair, airbrushed makeup, and gaudy silver jewelry, there is no mistaking it: You are nose to nose with the notorious Miss Texas. You've heard rumors that it was her mom who hired the hitman to get her on her high school cheerleading squad. Whether that's true or not, the old saying "Don't Mess with Texas" definitely applies to her.

"What are y'all doin' here?" she screams in her thick Texan twang.

"I'm just here to get drunk and fuck a trucker," you deadpan. Texas looks at you blankly and then bursts into snorts and giggles.

"You are too much, Vermont. You have to come sit at our table," she gushes. "We got last year's Miss Liberty with us," she adds with a wink. You look over to her table and spot Miss New Jersey, who is favored to win because her father is the union boss who built Daniel Aces's Atlantic City hotels. You also spy Miss Iowa, whose mother is said to be in cahoots with a few judges—*very* close cahoots. Finally, you spot last year's Miss Liberty, swilling a beer and checking out your buddies, unimpressed.

A sudden Machiavellian urge sweeps through you, and you really want to know what all the heavy-hitter beauty queens are doing here, and if you can benefit from any information they might give you. If you make it to the finals, 10 percent of your score depends on peer votes, and these girls are the kind who can influence the masses. On the other hand, do you really want to waste your night out with a bunch of hard-core pageant bitches? Your friends will never help you win this pageant, but they are a far cry from the obsessive creepiness of Miss Texas.

Then again, you did come to Reno to win this thing. . . .

Join Texas and her posse of princesses by turning to page 155.

Just looking at the caked-on mascara of Texas and Jersey side by side makes your stomach churn. Reunite with Nevada and your fellow small states by turning to page 15.

You never actually went to slumber parties as a kid; you only used them as a shell game so your parents wouldn't know you were out with your boyfriend. You figure this might be your last chance to see what they're all about.

"Sorry. The Miss Liberty Tequila Shooter Team's gonna have to go it without their ace tonight," you tell Miss Nevada. After a pout, she heads down the hall to meet the other girls. You turn to Miss Montana with a grin. "Should I bring my pillow and my favorite *Playgirl* magazines?"

"Oh, you sure are a crack-up! See you down the hall!"

You open up the door to your room, hoping for half an hour of calm before the pajama jam, but instead you find a familiar sight: your roommate, Miss Florida, crying her eyes out.

"Hey . . ." you say, trying to sound like this hasn't happened ten times in the last week, "are you okay?"

"Do I *look* okay?" she says between wheezes. Actually she looks kind of puffy and red, but you don't think that will cheer her up.

"The big day's tomorrow—you should be excited," you try, hoping she'll just try and at least act like she's normal now that you're in the room. No such luck. You gather up your pillow and your flannel pajamas (sadly, you haven't thought to bring any *Playgirl* magazines), but Miss Florida's still crying.

"My . . . life suh-uh-ucks . . ." sobs Miss Florida. She looks really bad, worse than usual. This is a girl with a ton of prescription pharmaceuticals and a mother who somehow slipped through the cracks of the Florida child welfare system. You suspect the great state of Florida was too busy fishing little Cuban boys out of the ocean and shipping them back to their oppressive homelands.

"So . . ." you say, wincing. "What's wrong?"

"It's *everything*."

Could she be a little less specific? You take a stab at the obvious. "You mean all the pressure, the pageant?"

"It's not fun anymore. My mother's been calling me nonstop, all night long. The only reason she's not in the room right now is because they ban coaches and parents from the floor the night before the finals. I can't take her anymore! You've met my mom, you know what she's like." Your impression of Miss Florida's mother is that she's like Joan Crawford on a bad day every day. Only she wields mascara wands instead of wire coat hangers.

"She seems like she means well," you try lamely. "You just have to find the fun in this. I mean, that's why I'm here." Then you add, hoping she'll take the hint, "That's what I'm going to do right now: have some fun. Down the hall. Pajama jam—"

"God. I don't even remember the last time I had fun at one of these pageants! I guess my best memory was when I was four, now that was fun—"

"*Four?*" you choke, nearly dropping your pillow.

"That was when I won Little Miss Cocoa Beach ages four to six." Her eyes mist over. You try to hide your horror. "Back then it was all so pure."

Okay, that's it. "You know what," you say forcefully, "you must be smoking some kind of SuperCrack if you think that parading around at a pageant at the age of four is *pure*." Miss Florida looks at you like a confused puppy.

"You were exploited as a child. Has anybody ever mentioned this to you?"

Miss Florida goes to her suitcase and brings out a photo album the size of a world atlas. She opens the cover and inside are hundreds of photos, all of herself, dressed to the nines at the age of nine. JonBenet Ramsey never looked this good. "Here," she says, "see how happy I look? How could this be exploitation?" You're about to launch into a tirade when Miss Florida starts crying again. You stand there for a moment, and then figure it's time to head for the door.

"Hey, hang in there, sport!" you quip, hoping for a smile.

"Don't . . . luh-luh-leave . . ." Miss Florida manages between sobs. "You're the only person I can talk to. All the other girls, they think I'm a freak, but you—you're not like them." You realize that nobody has ever said one sensible thing to Miss Florida. She needs you. And part of the Miss Liberty spirit involves watching out for your roommate. If you leave her in her time of need, who knows what she'll do? Order razor blades and Drano from room service? Then again, down the hall there's a bottle of peach schnapps with your name on it.

You've had some freak-outs in your life when you needed a good listener and a shoulder to cry on. Help Miss Florida return to her Sunshine State by turning to page 19.

You might help Florida and get some kind of karma reward in return, but that shit takes centuries to pay off! Ditch the roommate and go to the pajama jam on page 147.

You are afraid that too much time with Miss Texas could lead you to a night of line-dancing or an unfortunate aerosol hair-spray incident. Go hang with your girls.

"Thanks for the invite," you say. "I would love to join *y'all* but I am here with them." As you brush by Miss Texas, she grabs your arm and whips you around.

"I don't know who you think you are, tree-hugger," she seethes, her head swinging and her index finger wagging, "but you are about to go down."

"I don't know who you think you are, gas-guzzler, but here's a little newsflash: Silver dolphin pendants went out in 1990." With that, you push her aside and join your girls, Jack and Coke in hand.

You breathlessly recount the psychotic encounter with Miss Texas to a rapt table of beer-swilling pageant queens. They giggle with delight and share some of the dirty rumors they have heard about Miss Texas:

"I heard that she has a Mexican drug lord sugar daddy funding her trip here."

"I heard that she has a third nipple somewhere on her stomach, so I cannot *wait* for the swimsuit competition . . ."

"She's totally a man, baby! Have you seen the size of her hands? Hello!"

You are cracking open a can of Pabst Blue Ribbon, when you spot him—the rack-o-chips-expensive-shoe-hair-gel babe from the casino! What is he doing in a place like this? He slides in to a nearby table with a pitcher of beer and a stack of glasses. You watch his tanned forearms as he hoists up the pitcher and slowly pours himself a glass. There is no one else at the table, but he looks like he may be expecting someone.

"God that man is beautiful," you murmur to the girls. "I could eat him with a spoon." Slowly, they all turn around to get a better look.

"Mmmm, tasty for sure," whispers Nevada, "but he looks a little creepy too. Like he's too perfect, you know?"

"Yeah," adds Delaware, "like the Prep School Strangler or something . . ."

As the conversation turns to teeth whiteners and tongue scrapers, you cannot help but notice that Prep School Strangler keeps looking at you. You give him a little smile, and you swear you can see him blush. His table is still empty, so this is your chance. Besides, you've never been the type of girl to sit around and wait for a guy to make a move.

"Uh—I'm going to the bathroom," you say, taking leave of the oral hygiene conversation. You flip back your hair, push out your chest, suck in your tummy, and do your best pageant walk past his table without dropping a single glance his way. In the bathroom, you expertly apply your lipstick, drop Visine into your eyes without smudging your eyeliner, and rearrange your push-up bra. Jesus, you think, are these the only skills you have learned during the past year on the pageant circuit?

You glide out of the bathroom and spot his table in the distance. There is a pack of Marlboros on the table. Here you go.

You strut toward him, place your hands on his table, and say, "Hi—could I borrow one of those cigarettes?"

"Borrow? I don't know how you're going to give it back if you smoke it," he says, beaming at you.

"How about we just share one then?" you propose. He stands up, pulls out a chair, pours you a beer, and lights up a smoke, all in about five seconds flat.

"So, what brings you to this classy establishment?" he asks.

"Oh, um, I'm here with some . . . business associates. In town for a kind of convention thing." You would rather not disclose your embarrassing beauty queen secret so early in what will probably become a lifelong relationship based on trust and respect.

"Wow, what kind of business do you do?" Why is this guy so nosy?

"You know, sales, marketing, that kind of thing. . . . What do you do?"

"I manage hedge funds." You pretend to understand what that is. "My name is Ian."

You smile. "Of course it is." Ian seems an appropriately yuppie name.

He is charming and polite, but you can tell there is something devilish beneath the surface, and you love it. He places his hand on your thigh and rests it there. Wow, you think, he is forward, but he is smooth. Just as you are piecing together an imagined future with him—a beach house and a ski house, cuddling by roaring fires, and eating romantic dinners prepared by your own personal chef—you are roused by a tap on your shoulder.

"Hey sweetie," cooes Miss Nevada, "we have to get back to the hotel for some beauty sleep. Come on." You look up at her desperately, hoping to send her a psychic message to give you just ten more minutes.

"Or," Ian offers, "I could give you a lift. Or put you in a cab. Whatever you prefer." He smiles and you can feel your stomach drop a few notches. A few very good notches. You *could* technically stay for just one more drink—it wouldn't kill you and it does not mean you have to go home with the guy. Where are your priorities? What if he ends up being your future husband and you blow it for some dumb beauty contest? But are you really such a horndog that you will sacrifice sleep the night before you make your debut on national television? Hurry up, Miss Nevada is already halfway out the door.

The company of a sexy man has been known to give you a certain glow that actually may help you win this thing tomorrow! Stay for one more beer and turn to page 22.

Calm your raging hormones and focus on the real prize. You came here to win—so get your sweet ass back to the hotel and turn to page 55.

"Thanks for staying," your roomie sniffles. It's so pathetic your heart just sinks.

"You know, all those beauty pageants, all the contests, I don't think you did them for yourself. You did them for your mom."

"What do you mean?" she says, crinkling her face in confusion. "I have all the ribbons."

"What about the cash prizes? The charity money?"

"My mom used the cash so I could enter more beauty pageants. And the charity money—well, how else would I take those interior design classes at the community college?"

"Okay. Now, you're not serious, right?"

"Maybe it's not important to people in Vermont, but in Florida, we demand a home with matching color schemes and creative but muted touches."

"Did you just diss my state?"

"You're not *helping*!" she cries. It's like a flashback to junior high school dances. Walk into the girls' room and all you find are hordes of girls crying their eyes out into that cheap little toilet paper that only comes in individual sheets. Miss Florida is like that whole bathroom crammed into one girl. And they're playing "Careless Whisper," and it's her song. Perhaps this situation is a little more dire than you thought. One thing is for sure—this could go on for hours.

"I don't really know how to help you if you won't listen to

me." You're getting more and more frustrated. She's like a cult member! You once watched a show about cult deprogrammers. They kidnap the kids, lock them in a cheap motel, yell at them, and occasionally beat them until they break and promise they won't try to ascend to the mothership. You don't really have the time or the skills for that, and beating might cause you to break a nail, but this girl needs some kind of lesson in reality.

Right now, Florida is teetering on the edge of sanity. She's pacing. You know that she'll dash into the bathroom at any moment and lock you out. And you're not peeing in the ice bucket—not again, not like that time during spring break in South Padre your senior year. You shiver at the thought. There are two ways to handle this delicate situation: you let her cry her eyes out or you give her the reality bitch-slap. One is whiny and may involve your feeling a little guilty, but it does involve your getting some rest. The other involves you getting no sleep, yelling at Miss Florida, and finally having a tearful reconciliation. Too bad you can't just kick back and bond over that Shannon Doherty television movie where some stalker chick tries to ruin her life because the two of them were pitted against each other in child beauty pageants. You wouldn't mind seeing that again; it's actually a pretty good movie . . .

"You know what? Forget it," she sighs. "You don't understand what I'm going through. Everybody knows you totally lucked into this whole thing."

Okay. Are you ready to take off those little white gloves?

Throw down with Miss Florida and go off about how screwed up those child beauty pageants have made her. It's called tough love and you'll find it on page 31.

So what if she's sobbing? College taught you to sleep through an orgy. Get your beauty sleep on page 24.

Isn't the hope of meeting a man always the point of going out in the first place? You are staying with your guy and letting the girls go.

"I'll be fine," you tell Nevada. "Just one more beer, I swear."

She gives you a look like she doesn't quite believe you, and then the requisite peck on the cheek goodnight.

"How do you know them?" Ian asks.

"Oh, just through the sales firm where I work. You know, sales . . ." You trail off, and then randomly change the subject to the first thing that comes to mind: surfing. Being Miss Vermont and all, this is yet another subject, like sales, that you know nothing about. However, by the time your next round arrives he believes you're a wave-shredding betty. Actually, all this impromptu lying could come in handy for those interview questions tomorrow . . .

It only takes two more PBRs and thirty minutes of staring into Ian's blue eyes to convince you to leave with him. You walk arm-in-arm out of the bar toward his car. He leans you up against the driver's side door, wraps his arms around your neck, and delivers a scorching kiss. Your thighs burn and your tummy tingles, and you grab him around the waist and pull him in closer. You can feel him throbbing and pushing on your hips as he tilts your head to the side and whispers, "I haven't been this hard since I shot a thirty-two on the back nine."

You pull away and look into his clear blue eyes.

"Oh. Thanks."

God, you want him, but do you really want to wind up in someone else's bed tonight? And did he just compare you to golf? Maybe you can call him tomorrow after the pageant or something. You let another kiss decide. You pull him in again, and this time it's one of those full-body kisses where everything inside you goes liquid. Shit. The sex is going to be good. Really good. And you hate to admit it, but it has been a while for you. I mean, what are the chances of winning tomorrow anyway? If you don't make the cut, it could all be over in ten minutes. Your chance at an orgasm is much better, and that alone would make this trip worthwhile. . . .

You are going to have sex. With a cute yuppie named Ian. Just remember that name when you are screaming out in ecstasy, and turn to page 48.

There are a million reasons not to go home with him. You have a pageant tomorrow, he plays golf. . . . Call it a night and turn to page 27.

What the hell is it with Florida? you ponder. If they're not screwing up national elections, training terrorists to fly airplanes, or helping the Disney corporation make money, they're busy churning out pageant freaks like your roommate.

"Well, goodnight!" you chirp at Miss Florida. You make a mad dash for the bathroom, where you spend the next half-hour doing your prescribed skin-care regimen. Several cleansers, a mild astringent, a five-minute mask, and a moisturizer later you're ready for bed. The whole time you've been in the bathroom you could hear Miss Florida crying, and the guilt is almost as hard to deal with as your complicated skin-care process. You have to focus. Girls who win Miss Liberty simply don't have time to coddle the competition.

After a nice stretch of quiet, you emerge from the bathroom. Miss Florida has dimmed the lights, but you can tell she's still crying. God. This is straight out of summer camp and she's the homesick girl. Then you remind yourself that she dissed your state.

"Are you going to be okay?" you ask meekly.

"I just need to get some sleep," she replies, barely above a whisper.

You take the hint and switch off the light. All the worries in the world couldn't keep you awake—these pageants wear you down to the bone. After counting about twenty sheep you fall into the deep sleep you've been craving all day.

"Would you *look* at yourself?" a voice screeches like a harpy from Hades, making for a hellish wake-up call. "Puffy eyes, blotchy face, I've never seen anything so disgusting in all my life."

Say hello to Miss Florida's mother, Wanda. She's got talons for nails, shock-blue eye shadow, and bleach-blonde hair. She looks like the worst drag queen this side of Greenwich Village—only drag queens would never wear a fringed T-shirt.

"Good *morning*, Wanda," you say. "Aren't you banned until after the pageant?"

"Stay out of this, Burlington Coat Factory."

Did she just diss your state too?

"Mom, I'm sorry," whines Florida. "I was up all night crying and I didn't know what to do."

"Didn't know what to do? What do you think the Secanols are for?"

"They don't work on me anymore. You know I built up a tolerance in high school."

"I can't believe you have the nerve to disappoint me like this. After all I've sacrificed to put you through these pageants! Every penny I earn at the Chicken Wingdom goes straight to you, and this is how you repay me?"

This woman makes Tony Soprano's mother look like a

pussycat. You avoid the verbal attacks and race into the bathroom for refuge. Through the door, you hear your roommate pleading with her mother. The poor dumb kid, if only she had the balls to just tell Wanda to kiss her ass, everything might turn out okay. But that's not going to happen, and you know it.

Dreading your skin regimen, you stare at the wall. Then you see it: the bathroom phone. Only a few idiot millionaires have them, but more and more hotels are putting them in. It figures your bathroom would have one, since the guy who built this hotel is one of those idiot millionaires (pardon, idiot *billionaire*).

Florida's mother has obviously paid off some guard to let her up on the floor, since she's really supposed to be sequestered with all the other mothers. Can you imagine if they let your parents up here? You practically wept with joy when they told you the only time you'd have to see your family was after the pageant. Miss Florida doesn't have that luxury. All it would take is one call down to the Miss Liberty command center and Wanda the Wondermom would be escorted off the floor and out of the hotel. Of course, it's not your battle to fight. But you are the one trapped in the bathroom.

Isn't the bathroom phone a cosmic sign? Drop the dime on Wanda and get her kicked out by turning to page 79.

Miss Florida is a grown-up, even if her mother isn't. Let her take the hit and go to page 86.

Ian might curl your toes, but it's time to get home and curl your hair.

"I can't go back with you," you whisper. "I need my beauty sleep."

He pulls back, a look of scorn in his eyes. "What kind of cock-tease are you?" Hello Prep School Strangler . . .

"Look, I had a hot time with you," you begin, trying to calm him down, "but I have an early sales conference tomorrow. Maybe after that we can—"

"Fuck you, Vermont!" he cuts you off.

"What did you call me?"

"You heard me, Miss Vermont." He's in your face. "You come from a shit state full of potheads and chicks who don't shave their legs. I can't wait to see you fail tomorrow."

How does he know who you are? You want to question him, but right now your priority is getting to a well-lit area of the parking lot to find a ride back to the hotel. As you hustle to the bar entrance he shouts, "You were only worth five points, Vermont! Five, you sorry bitch!" Points? What is this, you wonder, some kind of game?

The entrance of the bar is steps away when you are nearly run over by a teal Geo Storm. The car screeches to a halt and you jump back, covered in dust. The windows of the car roll down to reveal Miss Texas, Miss New Jersey, and Miss Iowa. The former Miss Liberty is behind the wheel.

"Don't tell me," Miss Texas gloats, "you just got nailed in the parking lot by that pageantizer!" You stare at her in horror—what is a pageantizer?

"Girls of the lesser states like Vermont only get five points, though," Iowa adds. "Not enough to put him in the lead."

"Wow, he must have really liked you to waste his time," adds Jersey. "There is no way he'll catch up with Andrew. He nailed the entire Pacific Northwest!" Those bitches must have watched you flirting with Ian all night, knowing damn well that this was all some Spur Posse game. You feel dejected and embarrassed, and have the sudden urge to hurl and insult. In front of you is the perfect target. . . .

"Hey, nice Geo," you yell at them. "How much Camel Cash did it take to buy that?"

"Wrong," she replies. "I won it in Miss Liberty." With that, the car peels out and you are left, stranded in a Nevada dive bar the night before the biggest day of your life. You reach into your purse for your wad of cash, but only come up with dozens of beauty products. You remember that you handed your money to Nevada to pay for the cab ride, and never got your change. God, you are screwed. You could try to call your hotel, and maybe wake your roommate for help. But the way you treated her earlier was less than Miss Congenial, so you doubt she would lend you a hand. You could go back and demand a ride from the pageantizer, but date rape is not on your agenda.

You spot a bus stop on the edge of the parking lot near

the main road. You wander over to take a look at the map, and sure enough, there is a bus route that runs to the casino strip, right near your hotel. You scrounge around in your purse and find fifty cents. You're in business. It may take an hour for the bus to arrive and another thirty minutes of riding, but you'll be able to catch four hours of sleep before the pageant begins. You're wondering if the hotel convenience store sells Red Bull, and how many you will need to see you through tomorrow, when a pickup truck pulls up beside you. The driver unrolls the window and pokes his head out.

"Yer not waiting here for the bus, are ya?" He is an older man with gray hair and a sweet smile. He looks like that old farmer in *Babe.* "You could be here all night, ya know."

"Yes, I'm waiting."

"It's not safe to stand here," he says, his face soft with compassion. "Let me give ya a lift. I won't be able to leave in good conscience unless I help ya out."

You look at the sweet old man. He kind of reminds you of your grandfather. It would really be great to get back to the hotel at a somewhat decent hour, avoid getting caught by pageant officials, and sleep for an extra hour. You look down the deserted highway. Not a bus in sight.

But isn't the first thing they tell you in kindergarten not to get into a car with a stranger? Have you become so deluded in your year of pageantry that you forgot this basic rule?

"Come on, sweetheart. Hop in," he says, pushing the passenger door open.

If push came to shove, you could kick this old geezer's ass and drive yourself back home. Cut your losses, get in the truck, and turn to page 35.

You've heard too many stories about sweet old men with hatchets under their seats. Wait for the bus and turn to page 41.

Time for an intervention. You're the class-five hurricane and Florida's going to get ripped from the Panhandle back to the Keys.

"Come with me," you say in your most commanding tone. You grab her pageant scrapbook, and march her into the bathroom.

"What are you doing?" she mumbles.

"I'm gonna show you what your childhood has done to you, if you ever had one!" You open up the scrapbook and pull out a blue ribbon that reads MISS PRETEEN PRINCESS. "This is your first crush," you say, as you throw the ribbon into the toilet.

"Are you crazy?"

"You had a first crush, didn't you?"

"No."

"You did. And now he's in the toilet. Tell me about him!"

"He was Mister Young South Florida! I was in sixth grade and he had . . ."

"He had what?" You shake her. According to the cult deprogramming documentary, sometimes that helps.

"He had beautiful blonde curls!" Miss Florida runs to her photo album and turns to the Young Floridians Pageant section to show you his picture. Mister Young South Florida is every bit the budding gentleman. He has the face of an angel and a flowing mullet of curly blonde hair.

31

"And what happened to him?" you ask, even though you already know the answer.

"My mom said I had to stay away from boys in the pageants! I never told him . . . I never told him how I felt!"

You throw more pageant photos and sashes into the toilet. "This is every boy you could have had but didn't," you say. "And all because your mother held you back."

"But she loves me! She even paid for my temporary false teeth when my baby teeth were falling out!"

"But do you love yourself?" you ask. Miss Florida stares at you with tear-swollen eyes. She genuinely doesn't know. "When you're ready to tell me, you can come out."

With that bold statement, you walk out of the bathroom and shut the door.

"Let me out!" you hear, muffled. Isolation therapy. This was another thing that seemed to work in that documentary.

"Child beauty pageants are evil!" you shout.

"They bolster self-esteem and stuff!" she shouts back.

You sit against the door, turn on the television, and wait. It's five minutes before she tries again.

"It's just a performance!"

You roll your eyes and turn on Conan O'Brien. God, that guy's adorable. Maybe if you win he'll invite you on! Then he'll visit you in the dressing room and ask for a private swim-suit competition. . . . You're in the midst of your Conan sexual fantasy when you hear:

"Pageants are scholarship programs!" she tries, dispassionately. And twenty minutes later: "Learning about competition is essential for any child!"

You're beginning to wonder if this is the point where you "reach out." You're not really sure you know what you're doing because you have never known anyone who was in a cult. The closest thing you've seen is your uncle who's into Scientology. He's amazingly stable except for his constant insistence that *Battlefield Earth* is this generation's *Star Wars*.

At this point she's been in there an hour. "Okay," you relent. "Name one friend you've made while competing in a beauty pageant."

"Miss Vermont."

You open the door slowly. Miss Florida bursts out of the bathroom and hugs you. It's a little startling, but it seems genuine. You're even more taken aback when she starts crying.

"It's going to be okay," you tell her.

Miss Florida's a whole different person by the time you're up the next morning. She seems almost normal when you leave to get breakfast.

"Would you like to come and get a croissant?" you ask her.

"I have some reflecting to do," she says with a sad smile. It looks like she was up all night and hasn't slept a wink. But you think she looks better than you've ever seen her. It's not fake enthusiasm—it's real.

You're smiling to yourself in the elevator as the doors slide shut.

"Hold the elevator!" shouts a male voice. You hit the button just in time and he runs in. He's cute in a disheveled kind of way with hair that looks like he just rolled out of bed. He's wearing a tux with bad shoes and is obviously a waiter. "Thanks! You really saved my life. If I don't get up to the penthouse in ten minutes, I'm in big trouble." You're about to press the lobby button, but this guy is so nice and frighteningly cute and you're still on a deprogramming high.

"I'll ride up with you," you say. He pulls out a gold keycard and inserts it into the elevator panel.

"Were you on your way to breakfast?" he asks. "Because they've apparently got a feast up in the penthouse and I could get you in."

"Oh, I don't know. If I don't get downstairs I could . . ." You're about to explain that you could get in trouble, but you trail off, because this guy seems very down-to-earth, and suddenly you feel awkward about being Miss Vermont. "I'm supposed to meet my family."

"It's too bad. This is the best elevator ride I've had in a long time."

If you want to order this dish for breakfast, head to the penthouse and go to page 37.

You better join the other contestants who are pretending to eat a healthy breakfast. Take a rain check on the penthouse party and turn to page 103.

You never were one for public transportation. Give this old geezer the thrill ride of his life.

"Thanks," you say, climbing in the front seat of his pickup truck. "I'm staying at the Aces Casino."

"No problem," he smiles, and guns his engine. You quietly listen to country music and watch the industrial landscape whiz by. You're gazing out the window, trying to mentally prepare for your performance tomorrow, when you feel a sharp and painful blow to the back of your head! Your vision clouds, and your body slumps down onto the seat. Then, blackness.

You wake up on a small, uncomfortable couch in a dark room. A familiar old voice asks you if you slept well. You rub your head in pain and confusion, and realize that you are no longer in the clothes you were wearing the night before. Light fills the room, and you see that you are wearing a sequined evening gown. Your surroundings are unfamiliar; you are in a windowless room with low ceilings and exposed plumbing. There are photos of beauty queens everywhere, along with trophies, ribbons, tiaras, and scepters. A room full of exotic moths and a suit made of flesh would be less frightening.

"Rise and shine, Miss Vermont," says the creepy old pickup

man as he enters the room. "Time to walk the catwalk." He helps you up, and you are too dazed to resist. He leads you to a makeshift catwalk, hands you a bouquet of flowers, and dims the lights. A spotlight hits a disco ball overhead, sending little twinkle lights over the entire room. An applause track and a recording of the song "Endless Love" fills the room.

"Now walk!" he demands, taking a seat on the cot. You notice he is wearing a full-length evening gown with a hand-gun tucked into a Miss Liberty sash. "Walk!" he screams. You are confounded, scared, and disoriented. So you walk down the catwalk in your strange gown, bouquet in hand. Then you do something you swore you would never do if you ever got the chance to take the Winner's Walk. You cry.

This ritual goes on for days. You lose track of how long you are kept prisoner in the rec-room from hell. You are plot-ting ways to slit your wrists with tiara crystals when a SWAT team finally bursts in and rescues you.

By the time you get out of the hospital and the psychiatric monitoring program, it is three months later. Upon reenter-ing society, you discover you have become a national tabloid queen; it's the kind of scandal that puts Patty Hearst's to shame. You do rounds of interviews with Barbara Walters, CNN, and Oprah. You write a self-help book that combines survival and beauty tips. Years from now, no one will remem-ber who won Miss Liberty 2003, but they will remember you—"The Kidnapped Beauty Queen."

The End

Love—or at least blind lust—in an elevator would make your morning worthwhile. Besides, down in the breakfast room you're just going to have to deal with lots of stressed-out pageant girls.

"You think the coffee's better in the penthouse?" you ask.

"You better believe it is," the guy says with a wink. When the doors slide open on the top level, you're amazed that this place is in the same building as your tacky room with the lame hotel art. This is a palatial penthouse—tasteful wood paneling, antiques, classy people—everything you'd expect in a Manhattan high-rise, except it's right here in Reno.

"How loaded do you have to be to stay here?" you ask, impressed.

"You have to be loaded enough to own the hotel."

"No way. Is this the Daniel Aces Suite?"

"No, this *is* Daniel Aces's suite."

"Is he here?" you ask. There are at least fifty people in the room and all of them look stinking rich. You and your hot waiter are probably the poorest people in the room. These people have you beat by the tens of millions.

"Yeah, he's here," the waiter says dryly. So he hates the rich! You will rail against the aristocracy together, spending a penniless but noble existence sharing a tiny apartment that forces you to spend most of your time in bed together. . . .

"Look. I have a couple of things I have to take care of, but I'll meet you for a mimosa in ten. Sorry to abandon you."

"I'll just act like I belong here," you say with a toss of your hair. You've spent all year practicing your poise, now's your chance to apply it to a real-life situation!

Your cute waiter disappears into a sea of people and you head for the breakfast spread. After noshing on the best bagel you've ever had (and this will likely be the only thing you'll eat all day) you head over to the bar. A sweet older bartender pours you a mimosa and you realize there is not one person here you really want to talk to.

"So," you say to the bartender, "what's the party for? I crashed."

"All these people are here for the Miss Liberty pageant."

"Oh. They're not officials, are they?"

"They're sponsors, I think. People who buy advertising or put up the big bucks to say they're a part of it."

"I didn't know there was so much money in beauty pageants."

"You better believe it. That Miss Liberty is a cash cow," he says with a wink. He tops off your mimosa.

"Hey, you know that young guy you've got on staff? Incredibly blue eyes and bed head?"

He's about to answer when fear crosses his face. He straightens up his tie and gets serious. You follow his gaze. Oh God. Daniel Aces is heading toward you. That's the thing about money—you can't smell it until it's right there.

"Hey there, James," Daniel Aces says with an overly friendly tone. You notice the bartender's name tag reads JOEL, but Aces is clearly the kind of guy who would believe his own recollection over a name tag. "Fill 'er up."

Aces waits as Joel nervously fills the champagne flute. You try to look composed, thinking you'll get points for both style and personality. But now he's staring at you, expecting you to say something. This guy's completely intimidating. You've got to say something, but that something is bound to be incredibly stupid. Where's your wanton waiter? You're about to break!

"You're not a reporter, are you?" Aces asks.

"No. Why would you think that?" you say, trying not to sound conspicuous. But you do.

"Because I know every person in this room except you."

"I'm here with a friend."

"Who?"

"I don't want to get him in trouble," you say, thinking of rich-ass Aces kicking your poor noble waiter out on the street. But Aces keeps staring at you. Those hypnotic eyes! No wonder he was able to buy out half the property in Nevada! "That guy," you say, pointing at your waiter. He's halfway across the room, talking to some old lady, probably taking her order so that she doesn't have to use her walker to get to the buffet. Sweet.

"Oh. I see," Aces says with a smile. "If you don't mind, I'd love it if you'd meet me in my office."

"What did I do?"

"Nothing. I'd just like to get to know you better. You're the most stunning woman in this room."

Well. You can't decide how creeped out you should be.

Then again, you remember reading about how Daniel Aces started a modeling agency last year. And you can hold your own, even against this guy. If he tries anything, all you do is scream, run out of his office, and collect your out-of-court settlement check a couple days later. It would definitely pay better than winning Miss Liberty.

The rich are different than you and me, but that doesn't mean you can't celebrate diversity. Step into Aces's office on page 44.

Be the only participant in the Miss Liberty pageant who just says no to rich older men. Turn to page 63.

You would rather brave public transportation than potential molestation. Take the bus.

"I'm just going to stay put," you say, closing the truck door. "Thanks for the offer. Drive safe."

"Okay, missy," the old man says. He pulls his car back out onto the highway. As you watch him go, you notice a bumper sticker on the back of his tailgate. It reads: I ♥ MISS LIBERTY. A chill creeps up your spine. Could he have known you were a contestant and just wanted to get you in his car? Suddenly, you feel ill. First a pageantizer and now this. You didn't think anyone actually skimmed, much less *studied* those little Miss Liberty profiles that ran in the local papers. Suddenly, you feel like a marked woman.

You take a seat in the bus kiosk and dig around for your emergency cigarette. You had the foresight to steal an extra butt from Ian's pack when he wasn't looking. You spark up and inhale. The night is silent, and there is still not a bus in sight. After you crush out the cigarette in the gravel, you lean your head against the wall, close your eyes, and go over the opening dance number and your talent routine in your head.

The next thing you know, your eyes are fluttering open and you are blinded by sunlight. You shield yourself from the rising sun and realize that it's morning.

"Fuck!" you scream to no one in particular, "Double fuck!" You spin around and see that the roadhouse bar is deserted, without a car in the lot. You are trying not to panic, but you have to be onstage in a matter of hours, and all you have to your name are six lip-glosses and pocket change. You would give your Miss Vermont year's supply of Ben & Jerry's for a cell phone and a pair of shades.

Suddenly, like an apparition, the goddamn bus appears. You climb aboard, throw some quarters at the driver, and beg him to take you to Reno. Settling in, you do a quick self-check. A glimpse in your compact reveals you have slept up against some kind of graffiti that has left a mark on your left cheek. It appears your ankles have now fed half of the spider population of Nevada. You run your tongue over your teeth, which feel furry. You couldn't be any further from a beauty queen.

You finally arrive at the casino. You scamper up to your room, grab your utility-sized toolbox full of beauty products, and sprint down to the theater. You are disastrously late, but you may be able to pull this off—that is, if the pageant officials didn't notice your overnight absence and let you compete.

A security perimeter has been set up around the theater to discourage paparazzi, terrorists, or heaven forbid, perverts from entering the premises. You dash for the police barricades near the backstage entrance. Making a beeline for the stage door, you are tackled to the floor, the wind knocked out of you.

"I'm Miss Vermont," you manage to say, trying to push the 250-pound security guard off of you. "I'm a contestant!"

"This chick is no Miss Liberty contestant," you hear another security guard say. "She has scars on her legs and gang tags written on her face." They've seized your metallic cosmetics kit, handling it like it's a ticking time bomb. A SWAT team wheels over a device that looks like a small refrigerator, and they place your makeup case inside. Suddenly, you hear a boom, and a flash of light rocks the refrigerator box. Your makeup has just been detonated.

Now, there's no hope. The security team brings you to your feet and escorts you outside the casino, explaining that you—and your gang—will never be welcome in any Aces Casino ever again. Shit. And that's where you wanted to have your bachelorette party. . . .

The End

When else are you going to get to see Daniel Aces's office?

"I'd love to see your office," you say, trying not to sound too eager.

"Great!" he says with a smile. He then catches the eye of yet another rich old white man. "I've got to speak to Mr. Ford for a moment, but it's just down the hall. The only door at the end. I'll be with you in five minutes."

"Okay, thanks—" you start to say, but Aces is already exchanging hearty handshakes with the old guy. You look at bartender Joel. "If I need you as a witness in my sexual assault case I'll give you 15 percent of the settlement."

"Ah, don't worry. He's a good guy. I think," Joel says.

You take your mimosa and head down the long hallway. Soon the sound of the breakfast banquet recedes and all you hear is the sound of your shoes on Italian marble. The door to Aces's office is huge—he probably saw it at the palace of Versailles and paid them to tear it off its hinges and ship it to Reno. Inside, the walls are covered with paintings you've seen in textbooks. The furniture is the kind of stuff you usually aren't allowed to sit on. The door creaks shut behind you. You're alone in Aces's office.

The first thing you do is check out the view. You can see everything—Aces's other casinos, the city, the mountains beyond. Reno actually looks pretty from up here. Then you check out his desk, which is the size of Rhode Island. There are more drawers than you can count. Suddenly an idea occurs to you! You have to steal some of Aces's personal stationery. You open up a drawer, then another, then—jackpot. Creamy eggshell paper embossed with Aces's name. Could that be real gold leaf? You better believe it. You dig deeper into the drawer until you feel something strange. Before you realize it's a button, you've pressed it.

One of the paintings begins to move, startling the shit out of you. Behind it is a giant computer monitor of some sort. A panel pops up on the desk just as a keyboard appears. This is way cooler than NORAD, and probably more advanced. The monitor suddenly comes to life.

"Welcome," a computerized *Space Odyssey* voice coos. *"The last file you accessed was Miss Liberty Project. Would you like to continue?"*

"Uh, yeah," you say, joking.

"Thank you," the computer replies. This sucker is voice activated!

Suddenly things start appearing on the monitor. Flowcharts, money, advertising accounts, agricultural commodities, stock market options . . . and what connects them all? You gasp in horror. The Miss Liberty Pageant.

"What the hell is this?" you say to yourself.

"Miss Liberty Project," the computer says.

"But why?" you say. Then you try to be more specific. "What is the end result of the Miss Liberty Project?"

"Total world domination through national nutrition standards, fashion industries, consumer spending, and the ongoing struggle between the male and female segments of the population."

"So it's not just a beauty pageant pretending to be a chari-table organization?"

"The Miss Liberty Pageant finds its way into every corner of American society. That is why it is so influential," the computer explains. You're in shock. The Miss Liberty pageant controls the country?

"I think you've seen enough!" Daniel Aces shouts. You yelp, freaked out. How long has he been standing there?

"All those—all those people out there—are they in on this?"

"They don't know what they're in on. All they know is that if they support the Miss Liberty Pageant, their stock goes up and they get richer. Money is all anybody cares about."

"Is that all you care about?" you ask him, terrified.

"I prefer power."

"You don't know who you're dealing with," you say in your most outraged of tones. "I'm not just some pretty girl who stumbled into your party. I . . . am Miss Vermont." Aces gasps. "It's true. And I don't want any part of your vast con-spiracy!"

"Hold on now, let's not be rash . . ." He's sweating! You're so proud of yourself. Titans of industry can't stand up to this guy, but you can!

"Rash? I'm gonna bust this whole thing wide open. I know people who work for *The New York Times,*" you threaten, neglecting to add it's your old roommate from college who happens to drive one of their trucks on Long Island, but Aces doesn't know that.

"You don't want to do that."

"Oh, I think I do!"

"You keep quiet about what you've seen and I will personally ensure that you win tonight. Whatever goals you have for your year of service, I'll take care of them. You can be the most powerful Miss Liberty this country's ever seen."

This is a pretty attractive offer. With Daniel Aces in your pocket you can be set for life. Keep quiet by turning to page 58.

Screw Aces and his ill-gotten gains! You can end the oppressive reign of old white men! Expose the conspiracy by turning to page 51.

Get in the car with Ian, you little harlot you.

"Let's go," you whisper.

He kisses your neck, lifts you off your feet to carry you to the passenger door, and literally throws you in his car. He climbs in, guns the engine, and peels out onto the dark highway. Even though he's driving, he can't keep his hands off you. You cuddle up closer to him and lick his earlobe until little moans escape him. You slide your hand down into his lap, mostly just to see what's there. You don't want any surprises, after all. You stroke the ever-growing bulge in his pants, and you can see he is very appreciative. And nothing makes you hotter than a captive audience.

"Please," he begs, "please go down on me. Just a little. Please." Maybe it was the fact that he asked so politely, or the nostalgia factor of giving head in a moving vehicle (which you haven't done since you were a teenager), but you decide to give Ian a little ride of his own. You unzip his pants, and he positions his arms so you can bend over. You clip back your hair (an absolute must for a beauty queen), wet your lips, and take him into your mouth. He is moaning and gasping for air as you deliver one of the most scorching blow jobs in your repertoire. The very real threat of instantaneous death should an accident occur always makes for the most powerful of orgasms. You finish him off, lean back in satisfaction, and watch him try to catch his breath while you smugly light up a cigarette.

"I am . . ." he pants, "going to give you . . ." he turns and smiles, "everything. When we get home, everything." You tell him that would be nice.

"Is it okay if I drop you off here and meet you inside?" Ian asks, as he pulls up to the casino entrance. "I don't want those idiot valets stealing my CDs."

"Yeah, no problem. I'm going to grab a drink at the cocktail lounge, so I'll meet you there." You reach down to retrieve your purse off the floor, and notice the contents have spilled out everywhere. In all your fierce writhing you must have kicked everything over. You scoop up your many lip-glosses, credit cards, and keys and leave Ian after one more kiss.

"I'll be there in five," he says, peeling out, clearly in a hurry to get back to you.

Fifteen minutes later, you are nursing a gin and tonic at the casino lounge, still waiting for him to arrive. You wonder if you have the right bar, or if he said to meet him in his room. Maybe. Your lipstick is a disaster, so you dig in your purse for your compact. A strange piece of folded paper falls out of your bag. You don't recognize it as your own. It must be from Ian's car. You open it up to reveal a chart that kind of looks like a football pool. It's an elaborate grid with the names of all fifty states along the left side of the sheet, and various sexual acts listed along the top. In each intersecting grid-box, there are numbers, or points. You read along the top. "The 2003 Miss Liberty Pageantizer Point Sheet."

Holy shit. You now realize what this is. It's a game between Ian and his buddies to see how many pageant chicks they can score with. According to the pencil scribbling he made in the margins, Ian is running in second place behind some kid named Andrew, but scoring better than Mike and Matt. And if you are reading this correctly, Ian has earned ten points each for screwing Miss Maryland and Miss Mississippi, seven points for getting a blow job from Miss Illinois, and five points for getting a hand job from Miss California. You locate your state, Vermont, on the left side of the chart. You scoot your finger over to the blow job column of the grid to see you are worth: three points! Three stinking points! You are *so* worth more than that!

"Bartender, another gin and tonic. And you better make it a double."

And who says pageants aren't degrading to women?

The End

You're about to level the playing field! Aces can kiss your ass!

"You think I care about being Miss Liberty?" you say with a sneer. "You're going down."

And with that, you march out of his office. As the door shuts behind you, you're pretty sure you hear Aces freaking out, screaming *"Start shredding!"* Little does he know that this is one conspiracy that can't simply be shredded away!

It's an hour into the Miss Liberty pageant. The lights are hot, the cameras are rolling, and you have made it into the finals. You were favored heavily, of course, and you were helped by the fact that your roommate, Miss Florida, dropped out at the last moment because after your successful deprogramming she had to be hospitalized for "exhaustion." You know the truth is that her conviction and integrity made her quit, which gives you all the motivation you need to do the right thing. You know your only shot at exposing this whole conspiracy is during the interview segment. While all the girls are busy rehearsing their pointless speeches about saving kittens and the rain forest, you're ready to change the world.

". . . Miss Vermont!" is all you hear. You walk onstage, smiling that smile and waving that wave. The orchestra swells with brassy theme music. In the front row, shaking and pale, sits Aces. He looks scared. And he should be. You walk up to the podium where orangey-tan Roddy Topper waits with his little microphone. They'll all learn the truth soon enough!

"If you had one million dollars to devote to a charitable cause, what would that cause be and how would you spend the money?" Roddy asks with a calculated wink.

"Well, Roddy, I'll tell you what. If I had a million dollars, I don't know if I'd bother sending it to a charity, because all of the large charitable foundations in the U.S. are secretly controlled by the Miss Liberty Pageant," you say with a smile. The crowd gasps. "Unfortunately, I've come to learn that the Miss Liberty Pageant is merely a means to an end that keep rich old white men in power. It's a vast socioeconomic conspiracy spearheaded by Daniel Aces and his elite inner circle. They control everything—the agricultural market, the entertainment and media conglomerates, apparel and fashion industries . . . not to mention their sick plan to take over NASA. The only person who isn't under their sway is Bill Gates and that's because he has more money than all of them combined. This pageant is a front, and behind it is everything that is wrong with society!"

Silence. Dead silence.

"Cut the mike!" somebody shouts from the wings. "Go to commercial!"

"Listen! It's the truth! Just dig a little deeper and you'll see—" and then your voice cuts. They cut you off. The red lights on the cameras blink off. Bastards. "The truth is out there!" you shout at the audience. Uh-oh. Security's coming in from the wings. Then you hear it—a giggle. It grows. Soon the whole audience is cracking up, pointing, jeering, and laughing at you!

"We can do this the easy way or we can do this our way," says the buff security guy.

"It's a *conspiracy*! Are you all blind?! You're sheep!" you scream, desperate. This didn't quite go as you planned. Security grabs your wrists, pulling you off the stage.

You never made it to the end of the Miss Liberty pageant. Miss Texas won, that little tramp. You're sure it has everything to do with the vast sums of oil and aerospace money that Aces makes in Texas. However, your exposé did go out to the world live on national television, and your story is splashed across tabloids and talk shows. You've been dubbed the "Conspiracy Queen" by those clever assholes at the *New York Post*. Your friends back in Vermont think those magic mushrooms you were so fond of in college finally took their toll, and your parents insist you need psychiatric help.

It was a rough couple of weeks but you've got a mission now—you work with a group of guys who live in a Winnebago parked outside Area 51 in the Nevada desert. They kind of worship you, and your influence is growing. With their help and their kick-ass website design, you know that your conspiracy-busting message is spreading. Bill Gates even secretly gives you money once a month to fight the good fight. You don't ever really miss being Miss Vermont; you've got more important things to deal with. Like exposing secret societies like the Masons—the shadow government that has infiltrated everything from international banking interests to the easy-listening music industry. You just know they were the ones who created Muzak to pacify the masses and compel them to buy certain products. . . .

The End

You have only twenty-four more hours of female bonding to deal with. May as well save Ian for later . . .

You reluctantly push your seat back from the table and leave.

"Bye, champ," you say in your throaty, sexy voice, leaving him drooling as you saunter off, girlfriends in tow. You even do that cool trick where you don't look back at him while you walk away.

You exit the bar with your underdog state sistahs and light up one of the cigarettes you stole from Ian's pack. You pass it around in a circle outside the bar and the conversation naturally turns to tomorrow's pageant.

"Well, I think that the only reason Miss Iowa is here is because of her father," Nevada says. "Everyone knows he's golfing buddies with half of the judging panel."

"Oh my God," whines Delaware, "I bet she totally knows what the questions for the final interview are going to be! Bitch."

"Come on," you say, "we all know what the questions are going to be: gun control, the importance of education, or the role of women in modern society." They look at you in shock.

"How do you know that? Are you 100 percent positive?" asks D.C. like a junkie who needs a fix.

"Haven't you noticed that the questions are all essentially the same? They have been for years. Gun control may be a sticky issue, but it's trendy right now."

"Well, I know where I stand on all those issues then," says Delaware, dragging on your smoke. "I am totally against gun control, because that's a constitutional right and keeps the government off our backs. Everyone should have a gun."

"Except illegal aliens, because that's who the guns are protecting us real Americans from," adds Miss Nevada. You wonder when your underdog state sistahs morphed into the "Pat Buchanan for President" rally.

"And as for women's role in society," Delaware continues, "I have to point out that the main contribution women make, whether we like it or not, is to make babies and take care of those babies. End of story."

"Totally true," agrees D.C. "America wants Miss Liberty to have family values, not to be a dykey corporate type."

You are flabbergasted. You didn't know women like this still existed. You thought they all died out when Betty Friedan came to town and American women began torching their bras. The other frightening factor is that America may actually see these women spouting this nonsense on national television tomorrow, and it could potentially poison young and impressionable minds. You feel compelled to debate their beliefs, if only for their own damn good.

Then again, you know answers like this will *not* go over well with the judges, who are desperately trying to bring the Miss Liberty pageant into the next century. Any of these sexist and bigoted answers can only benefit one person—you.

Do you give your friends a lesson in Feminism 101? Start singing "I am woman, hear me roar," and turn to page 113.

Their ignorance only puts you closer to the crown. Keep your mouth shut, hope they don't have daughters one day, and turn to page 60.

You will be able to do more good for yourself as Miss Liberty than you would as a conspiracy-spewing nut, so you decide to make a deal with the devil. You'll stay quiet, but you better win this thing.

In minutes, you're set up for life. Aces gives you a secret Swiss bank account and you make it clear that you've got a very big card to play if he doesn't keep you happy. You were feeling bad about that cute waiter you left back in the breakfast room—until you noticed the Aces family portrait. The cute waiter is his son! He's no starving intellectual, he's just a rich young Republican who one day will grow old and look just as goofy as his dad. You liked him better when he was poor and worked in the service industry. Ugh.

"We're all clear on this, right?" Aces asks as he hustles you out of his office.

"If I don't have that tiara tonight, you're gonna find yourself in an orange jumpsuit on the cover of your own tabloids," you say in the sweetest way possible.

"And this year's Miss Liberty is . . ." host Roddy Topper says, ripping the envelope. You hope you've practiced your surprised expression enough to sell the moment. You squeeze Miss Texas's hand as you both wait for Roddy to tear open the damn envelope. Then he says it. ". . . Miss Vermont!"

"Oh, thank you!" you shriek, hopping up and down. Miss Texas hugs you in shame and defeat, and recedes into the background. Confetti rains down and the music begins.

"Look at her . . . your Miss Liberty . . ." sings Roddy. You wave to the audience through fake tears. Somebody puts a massive bouquet of roses in your arms and the former Miss Liberty puts that tiara on your head. You do a fantastic job of sounding grateful and crying like Gwenyth at the Oscars, but you know the real reason you won: He's standing in the front row, clapping and cheering like he's so proud of you.

"Thank you! Thank you so much!" you weep. But you know the real reason you are weeping is because you have just become one of those despicable bitches who wins dirty. And your kind of woman always ends up being pulled over with a syringe of liquid cocaine under the driver's seat, caught in an insider-trading scandal, or featured on FOX's *Celebrity Boxing*. So enjoy your year-long reign while it lasts, because when it reigns, it pours.

The End

You decide to bite your feminist tongue and let the rest of the baby states dig their own graves tomorrow. Besides, you need to get home in time to bleach your teeth . . .

"Wow," you say as you climb in the back seat of the taxicab, "you really have some interesting political views."

"Political?" snorts Delaware. "Don't tell the judges, but I'm not even registered to vote." Well that's a relief, you think.

You unroll the window and let the breeze flip back your hair. You take in the unimpressive landscape and prepare for the next day, making mental lists of everything you need to remember to bring to the theater tomorrow: makeup kit, curlers, adhesive tape, extra panty hose, emergency tampons, electric guitar, subwoofer, photo identification, industrial-size tub of Vaseline . . .

Suddenly, a microscopic object flies into your eyeball. "Fuck!" you scream, rubbing your eye frantically. Your eyeball is stinging like it's been burned by a cigarette ember, and it also itches like hell. The other girls tug at your arms, trying to pry your hands away from your face.

"No!" screams Nevada. "Don't touch it! You'll make it worse!"

"It's *killing* me," you whine. Miss D.C. takes your hands and makes you sit on them, as tears fall down your face.

"Oh God," she whispers, examining you. The other girls

lean over to examine your face, and then recoil in horror. "It's really swollen. Don't worry; I know exactly how to fix it. Just don't touch."

You nod meekly and whimper all the way back to the casino, silently wondering if you should have stayed for another drink.

You feel like a one-eyed pirate as the casino lights hit you and you fight the urge to snarl "Argh, mateys!" as the group scampers across the casino floor and shuttles you up to Miss Nevada and Miss Delaware's room. They lie you down on the bed and hustle around the room like an emergency response team, fetching ice, cold compresses, and Advil, and carefully placing pillows under your head. Twenty minutes later the swelling subsides, and you feel ready to return to your room. You thank all your friends for their medical treatment with hugs, kisses, and wishes for an "awesome" pageant tomorrow.

"Here," says Nevada, handing you two tea bags. "Just soak these in cold water and put them on your eyelids for ten minutes. You'll be like new."

"Wait—no," says Delaware, "this is the miracle cure. A secret weapon of mine for years." She reaches into a miniature cooler full of makeup and pulls out a baggie full of cucumber slices. "These really do the trick," she says with a wink.

"Wow," you say, "cucumbers and chamomile. We could have a tea party!"

"Get serious V-Tee! You are like One-Eyed Willy right now, and the pageant is hours away!"

You return to your room, exhausted and sleepy. Your emotionally fragile roommate is already asleep with a head full of curlers and moisturizing mittens on her hands. As you silently undress, you examine the healing foodstuffs you have just received. Where do these girls learn this nonsense? I mean, you have been reading *Glamour* magazine for all your life, but you have never raided your fridge for beauty products. You lie down in bed and sigh. So what will it be? Should you use the cucumber slices or the tea bags?

You have always been a fan of caffinated beverages—excepting booze, they are the best of all the beverages. Brew some tea and turn to page 66.

You remember some spa advertisement where a blissed-out woman had cucumbers on her eyelids. She seemed to know what was up. Get cool as a—well, you know—and turn to page 71.

A creepy old man invites you into his office? What is this, Hollywood? So he has money, but at least you have dignity.

"No thanks," you tell Aces. "I think I'm a little young for you."

"Oh, I wasn't quite thinking about me," he says with a charming laugh. "I was under the impression that you were here with my son."

"Your son?" you ask. He points to the cute waiter across the room and waves. You practically spit out your mimosa.

"Chad. You said he invited you."

"Oh, of course," you cover. The tux, the confidence, and you should have noticed he has his father's intense eyes.

"I'm so glad he's with a sweet girl like you. I told him to try and mingle with the girls in the pageant, but he won't have it. He thinks it's all fluff, that no woman with any sense of self-worth would be in a beauty pageant."

"Isn't it more of a charitable organization?"

"On the surface. But then again it's all about surface, am I right?" Aces chuckles in a between-you-and-me way.

"You betcha," you sigh, relieved you didn't tell Chad you're in Reno representing the great state of Vermont.

"Hey! You met my dad," Chad says, threading through the crowd. "This must be fate." He smiles at you and your knees go weak. You're sure it has nothing to do with how filthy rich he is, because you felt that way before you knew he was the heir to a real-estate and casino empire. Okay, maybe your knees didn't feel quite as weak, but there was definitely an attraction.

"I like this girl," Aces says to his son. "She's got poise. You can buy taste, you can buy education, you can even buy personality, but poise—you can't buy poise."

You get the sense that old man Aces has no shortage of aphorisms like that. He smiles at you, and then catches the eye of an ancient guy across the room. "Ah. That bastard from Texas is here. I gotta go grease the oil men." He winks at you and then vanishes into the crowd. You're left standing there with Chad, the new love of your life.

"He's a real sweet guy, your dad," you say, trying to sound casual.

"He likes you. And my dad never likes anybody I date." Date? You're turning pink; you can feel it in your ears. "Just so you know, I consider this our first date. Breakfast. We can go on another date for lunch, another one for dinner . . ."

"Sounds like you've got it all figured out," you purr.

"I know this sounds corny, but I feel like there's something going on here," he says, gesturing at the open space between the two of you. "I don't say things like that very often—to be honest, I don't have to. With my family's money, I barely have to say a word and women throw themselves at me."

"I had no idea who you were," you admit. "I'm a little embarrassed to say I thought you were a waiter."

He grins. "It's the tux, I guess."

"You probably wouldn't want to be with somebody who can't tell the difference between a tailored Italian tuxedo and a waiter's tux."

"You think I can?" he laughs. He takes your hand, sort of innocently. You feel a spark, and you're pretty sure it's not static from the Persian rug you're standing on. "I want to know everything about you," he whispers. "How does a girl like you end up in Reno?"

Come clean and tell him your true identity—you are the love of his life by day and Miss Vermont by night. Hey, your first impression of him was wrong and you're still into him—maybe nothing will change if you turn to page 69.

Screw that! Don't you dare tell the truth! There's a time and a place for everything and he's gorgeous and rich, so make up a story that doesn't involve the Miss Liberty Pageant by turning to page 75.

You decide to go for the tea bags. This way, you can eat the cucumber slices if you get hungry in the middle of the night.

You grab the teabags, stumble to the bathroom, and run some hot tap water. You brush your teeth, wash your face, exfoliate, dab on astringent, and begin your moisturizing regimen, which involves an organic "primer," an oxygen-infused lotion, and finally a heavy cream. You sigh as you soak the tea bags in a hotel glass, wondering how your life got this absurd. A mere year ago your skin-care routine consisted of falling asleep with your makeup on, then splashing cold water on your face to rouse yourself from your morning hangover. You examine your eye, and though the swelling has gone down, it's still slightly puffy. And if the camera adds ten pounds, then it can certainly add more puff to your eyelid.

You return to bed with the wet tea bags and check the clock so you can time the prescribed ten minutes. You're not as anal-retentive as your roomie, who has set at least three separate alarm clocks for tomorrow morning. You rest in bed and place the tea bags on your closed eyes. You do a few deep yoga breaths and mentally exercise "positive visualization." You visualize yourself in the opening dance routine, and banish all thoughts of stumbling down the moving staircase. You see yourself nailing your talent performance, a kick-ass rendition of Van Halen's "Hot for Teacher" on the electric guitar.

Just as you are drifting off, you dream of walking down the catwalk with your arms full of roses, a tiara on your head, and a massive check bulging in your bank account.

Clickety-clack! Clickety-clack! Clickety-clack-clack-clack!!!

Ugh. It must be morning, and your psychotic roommate must be practicing her tap-dance routine on the tiled bathroom floor. You open your eyes, but all you see is darkness. Are the lights off? Then you feel the wet stickiness on your eyeballs, and remember.

"Oh shit, shit, shit," you curse. You remove the tea bags and make a dash for the bathroom. You must have forgotten to take them off last night and—fuck! You shove your roommate—who is frighteningly attired like Shirley Temple on the good ship *Lollipop,* complete with sausage-curled hair and little patent-leather tap shoes—out of the bathroom.

"Hey!" she squeaks, "I wasn't done practicing! There's carpet out here and . . ." You slam the door on her.

You look at yourself in the mirror. Your eye sockets are a deep brown color. You try not to freak out, and start running some hot water. God, it looks like someone clocked you in the face. No, worse, you look like the lost daughter of Alice Cooper. You rinse your face with water, but the tea stains remain. You try soap, astringent, anything you can get your hands on—and with the arsenal of products in the bathroom, you mean *everything.* Thirty minutes of scrubbing later, you realize there is no way in hell you can compete today.

You emerge from the bathroom to be confronted by Shirley Temple.

"Oh my God," she says, her forehead crinkling with concern. "What happened to your . . . ?" You don't even hear the rest of it. You're too busy throwing on your clothes, grabbing your wrap-around shades, and stuffing your purse with all your remaining cash. At this point, there is only one thing to do—which is actually the thing you've been itching to do since you got to Reno: have a champagne breakfast at the casino bar, and spend the day playing craps.

The End

Honesty is the foundation for any relationship, and you want to build a big-ass mansion with a cement and steel foundation with Chad. You muster up the courage and tell him the truth:

"I have something I need to tell you," you say gravely. "I hope it doesn't change your impression of me. I've always believed that who you are inside is more important than what you do. Unless you're an assassin or something, which I'm not, but . . ."

"What is it? You can tell me," he implores.

"Chad, I . . ." you close your eyes, bracing for impact. "I'm Miss Vermont."

"What?"

"I'm here for the Miss Liberty Pageant. I got involved on a dare and now I'm here and I don't want you to judge me just because of this one silly thing."

"I don't think it's silly," he says.

You throw your arms around him in relief. "You don't? Oh thank you, I—"

"I think it's pathetic."

"Pathetic?" you squeak, pulling away.

"The Miss Liberty Pageant is nothing more than a bunch of women with a self-esteem addiction prancing around like show dogs. Every single time the Miss Liberty Pageant airs, the progress that women have made gets reversed by twenty years. And it's not just the pageant, it's people like you. So eager to be a part of it despite what it really *means.*"

"You can think whatever you want about Miss Liberty, but have a little perspective! That's not all I am!"

"Well, now it's all I see when I look at you."

"I hate to be so cunty, but now all I see is a prejudiced rich boy trolling for tail," you seethe.

You fling your champagne in his face. He should know not to piss off a girl holding a full glass. Although you're crushed, it feels great—you've always wanted to do that to someone. Everybody in your vicinity gasps. You just give them your beauty pageant smile and wave as you walk out of the party.

At the Miss Liberty Pageant that night, you barely even blink when you're knocked out in the first round. Everybody else is surprised, since they thought you had a chance to go all the way. But there's Chad, smiling like a jackass in the front row. You're sure that he fixed it this way.

When it's all over and you've had the "we're so proud of you" moment with your parents, you find solace at the bar.

"Hey V-Tee!" you hear. Sitting at a dark corner table is your roommate, Miss Florida. You grab two vodkas on the rocks and hand one to Florida, who was thrilled to be eliminated along with you in the first round. "This is it for us! No more pageants," she says, looking stable for the first time this week. "We lost Miss Liberty, now what are we gonna do with our lives?"

"We start living them," you say, raising your glass in a toast. You and Miss Florida clink glasses and down the drink. By the time your vision clears, you're both laughing uncontrollably, and you've made a friend for life.

The End

You decide on the cucumber slices—and now you can have a cup of tea in the morning to soothe your throat after a night of smoking.

You stumble to the bathroom and begin your extensive skin-care routine. God, part of you cannot wait for this nonsense to be over. Then you can toss out all of these tofu-almond scrubs, the apricot nectar salves, and the sea kelp toners. The first thing you want to do after this pageant is get really fucking sunburned—the kind of sunburn that results in tan lines, freckles, and heat rash. Then, you are going to smoke a joint and eat nothing but carbs. You settle into bed with the cucumber slices on your eyelids, which feel incredibly soothing. You drift off to sleep dreaming of Miss Liberty glory, and the debauchery that will follow once the whole thing is over.

The next morning you awake anxious and full of adrenaline. This is the day you have been waiting to arrive for an entire year. You glance over at your roommate, who is practicing her surprised "I won?" expression and princess wave in the mirror. You also remember that this is the day some girls have been waiting for since they got out of diapers.

You have two hours to get to the theater, which is cutting

it close with the beauty treatments you have to go through just to get your pretty ass out of the room. After a shower with various scrubs, exfoliants, and depilatories, you start a series of facial masks, do a last-minute pedicure and manicure touch-up, and dry your hair with a hairdryer, diffuser, and straightening iron. After your hair is stick-straight, you roll it up in a series of hot rollers, pluck your brows, pumice your feet (God knows what they will knock points off for nowadays), and get dressed. You have spent ninety minutes primping, and you have yet to put on a trace of makeup. By the time you have packed up all your makeup, dresses, shoes, musical equipment, and other essentials, you are out the door with twenty minutes to spare.

Like a nomad hauling your life on your back, you trudge across the casino floor toward the theater. Suddenly, you hear a familiar voice scream out your name. You whirl around to see one of your best friends from high school, Sarah, sitting at the casino café having breakfast.

"Hi!" she shrieks, running toward you. "Oh my God! It's been too long—what are you doing here?" The two of you were quite a pair of hell-raisers back in the day. She taught you how to shoplift 40-ouncers of malt liquor, and you taught her how to French-inhale cigarettes. "Come sit down and join me for a coffee."

"Okay," you say, "but I've only got a few minutes."

"So tell me," Sarah says, "what the hell are you doing in Reno?"

"Oh, well," you say bashfully, "I'm kinda here for the Miss Liberty Pageant."

"Holy shit, I knew it! So am I! That's so fantastic—I'm so happy to hear that you're on board!" You look at her, confounded. Sarah leans into you and whispers, "You know, I organized the entire protest."

"Huh?"

"It's going to be wild. We have hundreds of women from all over the country. We're going to storm the theater—and each woman is going to wear an outfit that illustrates how offensive this whole pageant is. We have a chick in a burqua with a sash that says "Miss Treated," a woman dressed as June Cleaver in shackles, and I am going to be dressed as a Madonna-whore—half nun and half prostitute."

You flush with embarrassment. Sarah points at the garment bags and cases beside you. "Is that your outfit?" she asks. "What are you dressing up as? I love the curlers—nice touch."

You feel so humiliated. Only a few years ago, this girl was one of your best friends, and the two of you were plotting wild exploits together—apparently, she is still plotting, only now to undermine the social patriarchy. And look what you have become: the embodiment of everything that liberated women rally against. You can't really tell her that your "costume" for her rally is a Richard Tyler evening gown, though your head full of curlers seems to have her duped.

Should you just come clean? The Miss Liberty Pageant has been working to make itself worthy of respect in recent years. It's not like you're in a Miss Hawaiian Tropic bikini contest, or a wet T-shirt contest at Hooters. Sarah has always understood you, so maybe she will understand that this is something you're doing for yourself and not an attempt to undermine your gender.

On the other hand, she sounds a bit militant. For God's sake, she got a chick in a burqua for this. You could just as easily excuse yourself to the bathroom and make a run for the theater. In the meantime, the clock is ticking and they'll be taking roll call backstage in a few minutes. . . .

If Sarah is a real feminist, she will support you in your quest for charitable and social reform, even if it means wearing a tiara. Come clean and turn to page 77.

You don't need this kind of pressure hours before you have to do a choreographed dance routine with fifty other girls on a moving staircase! Make up an excuse and get the hell out of there by turning to page 95.

You make a vow—this is the first and only time you will lie to Chad. But lie you can and lie you will!

"I'm here with my family," you say. Which isn't necessarily a lie, because they are here, after all. "They just love Reno."

"Where are you from?"

"Vermont," you say, treading carefully.

"You didn't go to Las Vegas instead?"

"Oh, no. They think Las Vegas is too crowded. It's not as classy as Reno."

He beams. "A girl after my own heart."

"I guess I am . . . after your heart," you say, wondering if that was as cheesy as it sounded. But he looks touched.

"Let's blow this joint. My family has a cabin on Lake Tahoe and I'd love to show it to you."

Okay, you've committed now. Make a lame excuse and it's all over.

"It just so happens my schedule's totally open," you say, visions of diamond-studded tiaras fading and dying before your eyes. "Do you guys have a boat and a private dock or something?"

He smiles, nodding. "You do have a swimsuit?"

"Oh, definitely," you say. You don't tell him it counts as 15 percent of your final score. Now *he's* the score.

You planned on staying with Chad for a weekend, but ended up staying for a month. As a birthday present, he bought you a vineyard so you could make your own cabernet. So you missed the Miss Liberty Pageant—the Miss Vermont runner-up was in Reno to watch the show and was so quick to replace you, most people barely noticed. And you have had to pawn some of your jewels to pay off friends and relatives to keep your pageant involvement a secret. Nothing works quite as well as a carefully constructed web of lies.

Most importantly, you and Chad were married in an opulent private ceremony, catered by Wolfgang Puck, with Harry Connick, Jr. providing entertainment for your guests, who included celebrities, captains of industry, and a certain undercover beauty queen.

The End

You have known Sarah too long to lie to her face. Besides, maybe she can promise to coordinate her protest to begin before or after—but not during—your talent performance . . .

"Look Sarah," you say, avoiding her eyes, "the bags are not my costume for your protest. They are full of evening gowns, prudish bikinis, Vermont-themed costumes, and about thirty pounds of cosmetics. For the Miss Liberty Pageant." All the color drains from Sarah's face. "I'm Miss Vermont."

Sarah reaches into her purse, pulls out a cigarette, lights it, and takes several long drags. A huge smile spreads across her face. "Brilliant!" she shouts. "Bloody brilliant!"

"I'm so relieved," you say. "I didn't know if you would understand. The whole thing started as a bet for several cases of beer—and now I'm thinking it could erase all my student loans . . ."

"Sweetie," she says, "you don't have to explain. Actually, it's perfect. Now you can use your position within the pageant to say some of the things we want to get across. It's the perfect platform to address some of the injustices women are facing today!"

"What do you mean—like in the interview part?" you ask, cautiously.

"Whenever!" Sarah answers. "It's live television. It doesn't matter what question they ask you, just speak about the modern woman's plight!" She smiles. "They can't stop you, and they know it. It will make them look like sexist pigs. It's brilliant."

"But," you protest, "I don't even know what your organization is about . . ."

"Vermont," Sarah teases, "here is a cheat sheet. Study up—make women everywhere proud. I'll pull the plug on the drag queens, burquas, and Barbie dolls." She slides you a pamphlet full of political goals and social statistics, and reaches for a cell phone.

You examine the propaganda and consider her offer. This really is an amazing opportunity to have the ear of the American public. You winning this pageant is not only unlikely, but it won't amount to anything if you can't make any positive changes as Miss Liberty. This may be your only chance to speak up and play a positive role here. Plus, you will guarantee a smooth pageant without a parade of radical activists.

On the other hand, you are going to look like a real nimrod if they ask you about the problem of world hunger and you start talking about equal pay for equal work. Plus, you have already invested thousands of dollars and hundreds of hours to make it this far. Can you throw it all away? You look at your old friend and her printed manifesto. Do you take it or leave it?

You have not waxed and moisturized and bleached and curt-seyed for the past year to screw it up now. Say no-thank-you to Sarah's political agenda, and turn to page 88.

Why not go down in a blaze of feminist glory? It will be a good story to tell your granddaughters. Fire up your girl power and turn to page 82.

You're trapped in the bathroom waiting for Miss Florida to grow a pair, and you can't wait that long. Plus it would be great to see Wanda banned from the premises, so you pick up the phone and dial security.

Now all you have to do is wait. You emerge from the bathroom with a half-smile, and float over to your closet to grab your things in case you have to make a run for it. Wanda has her head buried in your minibar, which they had locked for the pageant girls, but you get the sense Wanda's jimmied a few locks in her day.

"You make me sick," Wanda hisses at her daughter, swilling a mini-bottle of tequila. She lights a cigarette, noisily sucking down smoke like some disturbing creature from *The Lord of the Rings.*

"Mom, I keep trying and trying! One day I know I'll be good enough to deserve you, but right now you'll just have to be patient!" Miss Florida whines.

"Patient? I've waited twenty-one goddamn years for you to get to Miss Liberty! You think I'm not patient?"

Just then there is a knock at the door.

Wanda turns to you and her daughter and gives you the silent "shhh" signal.

"Who's there?" she asks in a fake falsetto voice.

"Security," your angels of mercy say. You're closest to the door and you practically run to open it. Several large men stand there in uniform. Behind them is the queen of the blue-haired pageant officials, Fanny Mae Briar. "Were you the one who made the report, Miss?"

You shoot Security Man a look that says "Oh God, this woman is crazy please don't tell her I called you," but he doesn't quite take the hint. You turn around to see Wanda has hidden behind the hotel drapes, but the smoke from her cigarette gives her away.

"Wanda, you're violating the rules," Fanny Mae barks. You better believe she knows Wanda. Everybody does.

"You!" Wanda cries shrilly, coming out from behind the drapes to point a Lee Press-On nail in your direction. "Ratted on by a tree hugging hippie!"

"I didn't have a choice, Medusa," you say calmly.

"You think you're going to win? You think you've got a chance to take Miss Liberty away from my little girl?" Wanda screams through a cloud of cigarette smoke. Security is slowly approaching her. Wanda clamps her cigarette with her graying teeth and grabs all the bottles out of the minibar. Unscrewing the tops, she pounces on your pageant clothes, which are laid out on the bed.

"Not the evening gown!" you yelp. You watch in horror as Wanda dumps the contents of the bottles onto your clothes in one fell swoop. Security makes a mad dash for her, but it's too late. Like some frosted-haired demon from hell, she spits out her cigarette. It falls onto your bias-cut silk Richard Tyler, and the whole thing goes up in flames.

"Burn, hippie, burn!" Wanda screams at the top of her lungs as security tackles her to the ground. She continues to cackle, giving you flashbacks to the "I'm Melting! Meeeelting!" scene from *The Wizard of Oz* that scared you so much as a kid.

"Mommm—you're embarrassing me!" wails Florida.

You stare in dismay as the room fills with smoke. By the time somebody can grab a fire extinguisher, it's all over. Your dress, your swimsuit, your best interview outfit—even your leather pants with the red flame stitching down the sides, which you had custom-made for the talent competition—are all one charred mess. Your dreams of the Miss Liberty Pageant have literally gone up in flames. You reach dejectedly for the one bottle of Crown Royal that Wanda missed, and swig it down.

And you will need that liquid courage to be the only Miss Liberty contestant to compete in each category wearing nothing but a complimentary hotel bathrobe. This may have helped your Van Halen guitar solo in the talent portion, but it got you disqualified in the eveningwear competition. The final insult came when you checked out of the hotel and four security guards confiscated the robe, but not before they caused a scene in front of your disappointed parents.

The End

Miss Liberty is supposed to be about the women who best represent American women—and a lot of American women are pissed off and mistreated. It's time they had a platform!

"Sarah, only you could convince me to roadsurf on the roof of your station wagon, and only you could convince me to make a mockery of a pageant I have worked my ass off to win." You grab one of her cigarettes and spark it up. "Fuck this misogynistic cattle show and the patriarchs who profit from it!" You take a long drag of the smoke and your face softens as you look to Sarah for approval. "Does that sound okay to you? I mean, do I sound convincing?"

She giggles and rolls her eyes. "Okay, Vermontie. Here is the plan . . ."

Several hours later, you are having the pageant of a lifetime. You managed to sashay across the stage in the opening number with a giant sculpture of the Vermont dairy cow on your head, and you didn't even get mowed down by the gauntlet of moving staircases. Plus, your talent performance stole the show. After Miss Texas twirled flaming batons, Idaho backflipped on a trampoline, and New Jersey did her best Celine Dion (and honey, even Celine doing Celine's best is painful), you dressed in flame-stiched leather pants and a torn sequined shirt and rocked the house with your rendition of the guitar solo from Van Halen's "Hot for Teacher." (How's that for progressive?) You were pushed-up and perky for the swimsuit competition—and watching the judges scrutinize your tummy and thighs with a critical eye made you more determined than ever to speak up against the sexist nature of the pageant.

Now, under the hot spotlights, you are the last in a row of five finalists who are being questioned for the "interview" segment of the competition. As if any real interviews consist of a single question. This is the part most contestants lose sleep over, because it requires them to think. You can vaguely hear Miss California drone on about how sad it is that white tigers are going extinct. You try not to roll your eyes. I bet she's not concerned about the *ugly* extinct animals, you think. It's so typical, everything is about beauty. Your feminist fire is growing. . . .

"What is the most dire problem in the educational system in America today?" the emcee asks Miss Texas.

"Not enough minorities are getting a fair education," she begins, "and that's because they don't really get to set foot in a schoolhouse door, 'cause they're too busy raising their illegitimate children." You try not to drop your jaw as she continues, "By minorities, I mean Mexicans and Blacks, and not really Asians, because they are brainiacs and also they almost count as white. And that's the biggest problem in education today. Thank you." You give a look that says "I'm sorry" to Miss New York, the Korean girl standing next to you. God, you are humiliated to be part of this nonsense.

Finally, it's your turn. "Miss Vermont, family values are an important issue in politics today. In your mind, what are 'family values,' and how do they help or hinder American society?" You take a deep breath and look out into the blackness. Out there are thousands of audience members and dozens of television cameras beaming you live across the globe.

"Until the antiquated structure of the American family is destroyed, women will always be treated as childbearing machines, unpaid nannies, and an invisible class of 'homemakers,' and men will continue to be regarded as powerful leaders and breadwinners. Our children are growing up in an inequitable and inhospitable society. Our daughters' values are not values at all. Instead, they breed, beautify, and educate themselves only to become more attractive chattel to the oppressive ruling class of men in America."

The silence and tension in the air is palpable. Roddy Topper starts to pull the microphone away from your face, but you're quicker than that old man. Raising your voice, you finish, "In short, the concept of family values exists merely to keep women out of our supposedly free society and barefoot in the proverbial kitchen. And Miss Liberty supports these antiquated values by staging this cattle-sale of a pageant. Thank you."

Roddy looks at you like you've just grown scales. You see that one judge has dropped her pen in shock. You are pretty sure that the next Miss Liberty will consist of contestants who intend to tour elementary schools lecturing on white-tiger habitats.

Moments later, as anticipated, you are dubbed third runner-up (read: loser) when the awards are announced. You are, however, the only contestant stalked by book publishers, progressive magazines, and radio talk-shows for weeks after the pageant ends. You and Sarah start an organization to empower young women, and your message begins sweeping the nation. Not one white tiger was saved during Miss California's reign as Miss Liberty, but dozens of young feminists were born.

The End

Just wait it out. With Wanda outside the door, you kind of feel like you're trapped in a bomb shelter. Who knows what it will look like out there when you emerge?

After about an hour of Wanda yelling, you decide it might be best to make a break for it. Miss Florida is in that silent sobbing part of the fight, and Wanda is in that smoking-two-cigarettes-at-once part of her assault. Even the best have to regroup in their corner after every round.

"Bye! I'll see you backstage!" you say, not waiting for a response. If college taught you anything, it was how to gather all your things and escape from a bedroom in sixty seconds flat.

After a breakfast where nobody actually eats anything, there are rehearsals all morning. You can cut the stress with a knife. The opening number is going to be a nightmare. Not only do you have to dance around with a giant cutout of the state of Vermont, but also there are these complicated moving stairs, the irritating Roddy Topper singing the Miss Liberty song, and lights so bright they could melt what is left of the polar ice caps.

During this whole time, you only catch a few glimpses of Miss Florida going through the motions. She looks okay, if a little dazed. You don't get a chance to talk to her until you catch her in the wings during the final run.

"That was pretty brutal this morning. You doing okay?"

"I need your help," she whispers, looking around. She leads you into an isolated corner, away from prying ears. "I'm going to lose."

"Is this one of those 'do I look fat' things? Because I hate compliment-fishers."

"No, I mean it. Miss Liberty is going to be my kamikaze run. Screw my mother. I'm gonna go down in a blaze of glory."

"How?"

"I need your help. You know how I'm doing 'On the Good Ship Lollipop' for my talent?"

"Sure, I remember," you say, trying not to point out that she's been singing those songs at the top of her lungs every free moment. "You even have that ship prop with the cute little smokestack—"

"That ship's going down." Miss Florida takes a can of lighter fluid from her bag. "A little bit of this and the whole thing disappears faster than the *Lusitania*."

"Wow, you know what the *Lusitania* is?"

"I need your help. Somebody's gotta stand watch."

This is a positive sign on the part of Miss Florida. Maybe she needs your support right now, even if it involves sabotage. Help sink the good ship by turning to page 98.

The last thing you want to do is jump on this girl's crazy train. Remind her that kamikaze pilots work alone and turn to page 91.

You came all the way to a tacky hotel in Nevada to win this thing. There is no way a guilt trip from an old friend will let you sabotage your chances.

"I just can't go through with it, Sarah," you say. "I really think I could use the prize money, and I've already come so far."

"God, you have changed," she says, with traces of pity and contempt. "We used to make fun of the high school cheerleaders. Now you are one."

That was below the belt. You gather up your bags, mumble a good-bye, and head off to the theater. Judging by the tight security, you figure there is no way Sarah and her army of militant feminists would make it past the box office. You suddenly feel relieved, and smile to yourself. I mean, come on. What did she expect you to do? Get yourself thrown out of the pageant for pulling a women's rights banner out of your swimsuit?

You greet your fellow contestants and sit down in front of your lighted mirror to begin forty-five minutes of zen-like makeup application. Your tension washes away and you channel positive thoughts for your performance. This is the time of the pageant that you love. While the gaggles of women from different states are running around all atwitter, you become calm and steady. You look at yourself through heavily mascara-ed eyelashes and silently tell yourself that you are going to win this fucking thing.

The dreaded opening dance number conquered and your talent number nailed, you are pretty sure you are in contention for one of the final five spots. The only obstacle that remains is the swimsuit competition. You are standing in the wings with a hideous turquoise bikini sticky-sprayed to your ass, and clunky silver heels you would never wear with a bathing suit. If you can make it through this little exercise, meant to judge your "physical fitness," you are home free. You hear your name announced. Throwing your shoulders back, you suck in your tummy, flash your megawatt smile, and strut onstage.

There are peals of applause from the inky darkness beyond the footlights. You are halfway across the stage when the applause gives way to horrified gasps. You instinctively know something is awry. At first you worry that something has popped out of your swimsuit, but your peripheral vision tells you that everything is in place. You smile and continue to walk, but then the houselights of the theater are raised. You stop dead in your tracks, in shock.

Out in the audience are several women in costumes. Actually, a couple of prominently placed women are not in costume at all—they aren't wearing a stitch except for sashes that say things like "Miss Bulimia" and "Miss Anorexia." Among the women are a drag queen whose sash reads "Miss Thing," a very obese woman whose sash reads "Miss Invisible," a cheerleader with a sash that reads "Miss Led," and a butch-looking biker chick whose sash reads "Miss Understood."

They are chanting and singing and locking hands in feminine solidarity. Suddenly, it doesn't matter that you were an honors student, a soccer player, and an electric guitarist. You feel like a cow at a cattle sale. You feel like a false golden idol, unworthy of praise and worship. Your shoulders slump, you stop tucking your tummy and ass, and your head sinks low. You want to run offstage, but it feels like your feet are glued to the floor. You slump down on the stage in humiliation. There you are, on national television—a broken beauty queen.

The End

***This is not the time to be seen helping Florida burn-baby-burn.
You have your own issues to worry about.***

"You know what? Good luck." You pat Florida on the head
and try to run away while trying not to look like you're running away. The only mistake you make is looking back—
because that lost expression on your roommate's face is a
cry for help.

The rest of the afternoon goes as planned, but you feel a
little off. You're never quite in step or in tune. You've done a
couple plays in your youth, and no matter how bad things
were, the dress rehearsal always went well and you could
always feel it *gelling*. But now, with all these girls, you don't
have that sense. There's an air of negativity, and everybody
feels it. You know why. Miss Florida—your roommate—is the
fly in the gelling ointment. Like Tonya Harding after her
"skate broke" in the Olympics, she's thrown several tantrums,
each one bigger than the last.

"Ladies and gentlemen!" shouts your host, Roddy Topper,
who should be shot for his spray-on tan alone, never mind his
voice . . . "Your Miss Liberties!!"

"We are all pieces of Lib-er-ty . . ." you sing, cringing,
"pieces of our so-ci-e-ty . . ." You sing it out—holding that
stupid Vermont cutout. All around you are the clomping
feet of the other girls, the stench of melting makeup, and

the glistening of stress-induced sweat. When you finish that god-awful number and march offstage, the only thing you can be grateful for is that you made it up the stupid stairs. Roddy is moments away from calling out the semifinalists and you're on the fringes, along with Miss Puerto Rico and Miss Guam, and who can blame them for feeling left out?

"Hey, Vermont," you hear from behind you. It's Miss Florida. She looks like shit.

"Hey. You looked great out there," you chirp, trying to sound perky. "You panhandle states are really at a disadvantage with the cutouts but you totally pulled through and—" It's right then that you feel the gun barrel between your ribs. She shoves you out onstage, much to the stage manager's dismay.

"Everybody listen up!" Miss Florida shouts. Roddy, hands on the semifinalist envelope, looks startled. Miss Florida holds up the gun and waves it around wildly. The audience gasps, and some start for the doors, screaming. "I want that tiara and I want it now! If it's not on my head in sixty seconds, this girl is going to be Vermont roadkill!"

"Do it!" you yelp. "This bitch is off her nut!" Everybody's rushing around, but the bright stagelights are blinding you. It looks like they're actually getting her the tiara.

"Look," you whisper, "this isn't winning. After everything you've done, everything you've worked for, you can't end it like this!"

"It was all bullshit. You taught me that. So I have a closet full of prizes and trophies—that's all they are. Symbolic scraps of plastic and metal and so much colored ribbon."

"Then—why do you need the tiara?"

"I just *do*!"

"No! You don't."

The audience is hanging on your every word. The cameras zoom in, broadcasting your hostage drama as it unfolds. You wonder if Florida just might back down, when, right at that moment, the pageant officials appear next to you onstage. They've got the tiara. They even have the "Miss Liberty" sash.

"And *you're* gonna crown me!" Florida growls at you.

"Somebody gimme that stuff!" you say, holding out your hands. Everybody's afraid to get close, because the homecoming queen's got a gun. Roddy, playing the reluctant hero, hands you the sash and tiara. You can feel their weight, and it is pretty impressive.

"Do it! I'm Miss Liberty! *I'm* Miss Liberty!" Miss Florida pants hysterically. She looks at the tiara, eyes gleaming. For a moment, it's not her face you see. You see . . . Wanda.

"Never!" you scream. In one swift motion, you swing the tiara at Miss Florida's head and connect, clocking her across the jaw. Rhinestones fly as she reels back, stunned. The gun drops from her hand—you now see it's the prop revolver Miss South Dakota uses in her *Annie Get Your Gun* number. The whole audience is suddenly on its feet, applauding. You don't know how to react for a moment, and then you turn to them and put your fists in the air, like you're Muhammad

Ali in heels and a cocktail dress. Roddy Topper takes your right hand, playing ref. Then he sings it out at the top of his lungs:

"Here she is . . . oh so pretty . . . our Miss Liberty . . ."

You can't stop smiling. For the first time in history, Miss Liberty has been decided by knockout.

The End

Make a mad dash for the stage door, you wimp.

"Um, I have to go find a pencil. I'm like, really into Keno," you mutter as you gather your things. "I guess we should catch up later." You bolt out of the café. You shake your head, disgusted with yourself, and wonder when your life became so humiliating that you were forced to flee childhood friends.

You walk through the stage door into a surprisingly quiet dressing room. You figure the rest of the girls are still up in their hotel rooms beautifying themselves to the teeth before arriving. You plop your things down in front of a vanity mirror plastered with Vermont paraphernalia. You look at your reflection surrounded by images of your home state—Ben & Jerry's ice cream, ski resorts, a VERMONT IS FOR LOVERS bumper sticker, and a photo of your family. It has been a long week of bullshit, and you feel a pang of homesickness.

Suddenly, you hear a deafening bang. It sounds like someone has knocked over a set piece. You spin around and hear a rustle of movement coming from the talent-competition equipment closet on the far end of the dressing room. Holy shit—someone is sabotaging the talent-competition equipment! My God, Idaho's trampoline is in there, Ohio's chainsaw for ice-sculpture is in there, and your amplifier is too! You feel an adrenaline rush and are overcome by a Nancy Drew–esque urge to nab this saboteur. You make your way across the room with great stealth and swing the door open. What you see next will be burned on the back of your eyelids for eternity. . . .

The ass of a naked, wrinkly man thrusts enthusiastically, while his voice barks orders like, "Oh yeah, baby! Give it to daddy!" You cover your mouth, attempting to silence your horrified gasp. Suddenly, the man turns his head, and you realize it's Roddy Topper, cheeseball emcee of the pageant, talk show icon, and infomercial spokesman for Tan-in-a-Can. He steps aside to reveal one Miss California down on her knees, jaw slack for a reason completely different than the one that is making yours hang open right now. Before you can run away and wash your eyes out with soap, Roddy zips up his pants and grabs you by the shoulders. He stammers the requisite line, "This is not how it looks . . ."

"How it looks?" you ask incredulously. "It looks like you're getting a hummer from the Golden State!" Miss California is up on her feet now, wiping her lips and swearing under her breath.

Roddy gives you his famous crinkly-eyed grin and begins, "I'm sure we can work something out here. There's no reason for us to act rashly. We can arrange a compromise."

You don't know how to react. Your *Charlie's Angels* instinct is to do some sort of judo kick and hightail it to the authorities. What do you have to lose? You now know that California has the rest of the competition licked, so to speak.

On the other hand, Roddy is a very powerful man. Perhaps you can hear him out and see what he has to offer. If California's playing dirty, then you can too.

Roddy could never give you as much as he's taken from you now that the image of his quivering ass has been burned into your brain. Run to the pageant police and turn to page 105.

You feel pretty confident negotiating with Roddy now that you've seen his rod. Find out what this pervert can do for you and turn to page 101.

You can write this one off as intense therapy for your roommate, although you're not exactly licensed for it. You take a look around. Coast clear—time to slash and burn.

You find the prop room strangely unguarded. It's probably because of the announcement made a few minutes ago, about some sort of press photo opportunity involving talent scouts, which nearly caused a stampede.

"Hold this," Miss Florida says, handing you the lighter fluid. She digs into the props, moving things out of the way so she can reach the Good Ship. You see Miss Montana's stuffed bull and lasso (the girl makes Will Rogers look like an amateur), the giant block of ice Ohio uses for ice-sculpting, Miss Hawaii's elaborate karate set-up, and then—finally—a pathetically decorated rainbow-colored ship. Ugh. You shudder. The portholes are painted to look like swirly lollipops.

"So. Mom help you paint this?"

"No way, we had it specially made. It's custom. Mom took out a third mortgage on the trailer to pay for it."

You help your roommate drag the ship out of dry dock, into an isolated corner of the room. There isn't much flammable around here—just a lot of concrete.

"You sure you want to do this?" you ask, making sure there's nobody around.

"More than anything," she whispers. She spritzes the

Good Ship with the lighter fluid, and then stops. "More than *anything*!!!" she screams, dousing it. You step back, a little freaked.

"Calm down, tiger. I think it'll catch."

"Shit. I don't have a light. Do you?" she asks. Your emergency match and cigarette flash to mind.

"In my makeup case, hidden in a tampon wrapper. A Marlboro and a blue-tip match."

"I'll be right back," she says with a grin. You stand there, can of lighter fluid at your feet, vowing to avoid the state of Florida for the rest of your life. The room reeks of lighter fluid, and you know this whole thing is going to go up and you're both going to lose your eyebrows. . . .

"What's the meaning of this?" a shrill voice rings out from behind you.

Oh crap, you think.

"Aren't you the Vermont girl?" It's the Nazi prop woman. She resents you already, mainly because you refused to let her handle your twelve hundred-dollar red Gibson Flying V guitar and she took it personally. "Is that lighter fluid? *Security*!"

Before you know it, half of the staff and most of the girls are surrounding you. The scene looks pretty grim—you standing over your roommate's Good Ship Lollipop with a can of lighter fluid.

"It wasn't me. I swear. Just ask my roommate—" In the crowd, you see her. She has a blank look on her face and what looks like a tampon in her hand. "Tell them what happened," you plead.

She looks around and approaches you carefully. With a red

face, she says, "I thought we were friends. I can't believe you would betray me like this." And she begins to cry.

You know when it's time to quit. And now is not that time. You grab the "tampon" out of that bitch's hand and tear into it. You light the match with your teeth, put the cigarette in your mouth, and light up. You exhale the slightly stale but oh-so-sweet smoke and stare at the lit match.

"Don't do it!" the prop lady warns. Everybody holds their collective breath.

"With Miss Liberty and justice for all," you say, turning away. Then with a glance at Miss Florida, you toss the match back over your shoulder. Whoosh! You can't actually see the burst of flame, but you feel its heat and hear the screams as you walk away, cool as ever, but banned from all things Miss Liberty for life.

The End

Let Roddy make you an offer you can't refuse, and he better not offer a lifetime supply of Tan-in-a-Can.

"Okay, Roddy," you say in your best don't-mess-with-me voice, "you have two minutes before I go to *The National Enquirer*. Start talking."

He chuckles nervously and runs his fingers through his silvery hair. "You seem like a smart girl. What if I offer to pay off your college loans?"

Not bad, you think, but the first rule of negotiation is never accept an initial offer. You look at him squarely and say, "I have money, honey."

"I could put you in my next infomercial. It's for spray-on nylons. It's the wave of the future! And you'll be on *television . . .*"

Television. Huh. "You know what, I do have an idea," you say sweetly. "I think this is going to be the beginning of a beautiful partnership."

One month later, you are sitting on a tasteful couch on a darkened soundstage, a coffee mug in hand. It's full of Red Bull, which has become your life blood since you started waking up at 4:30 AM. A makeup lady presses powder onto your face and tucks away a few stray hairs. Roddy takes a seat on the couch next to you and fiddles with his micro-phone. The stage lights begin to rise, and a cameraman in front of you yells, "We're on in five, four, three . . ."

"Good morning, everyone!" you chirp energetically.

"Good morning!" Roddy yells.

Then in unison, "Good morning!!!"

A smile is plastered on your face as Roddy begins his open-ing monologue. But your smile is not false. Since you talked Rod (as you now call him) into firing Cricket McCall, the blonde chipmunk of a co-host on *Good Day, America,* and hir-ing you as her replacement, your life has pretty much kicked ass. You have relocated to Manhattan, and the show has set you up in a swanky postmodern loft down in Soho. You are making an ungodly salary, not that you need the cash, because the show is also bankrolling your account at Bar-ney's, for any "wardrobe essentials." Even though you have to wake up before the sun hits the sky, you only work for a few hours and have the rest of the day to pursue your hobbies of shopping for midcentury furniture, getting massages, and accepting free cocktails from men who ask, "Aren't you on that television show?"

The End

There's no way you're getting sidetracked from your goal. Let the waiter take the elevator, you'll take the stairs.

"Thanks for the offer, but I've got a pretty full day."

"What, don't tell me you're one of those stuck-up pageant chicks?" he says with a condescending laugh, thinking you're in cahoots.

You step off the elevator. As the doors are closing, you give him a dazzling smile. "I'm Miss Vermont, jackass."

"Oh, shit, I'm sor—" is all you hear as the doors shut. Okay. Now where are the stairs? You quickly find them down the hall and behind the icemaker. By the time you're at the mezzanine level, you're out of breath. You swing open the service door and find yourself at the ass-end of a long hallway.

This is one of those floors full of conference rooms, which are only used during conventions and events like Miss Liberty. It's the dirty underbelly, the rooms where the judges talk shit and the pageant sponsors spew bullshit. But there doesn't seem to be anybody around. You poke your head into one of the rooms. Totally empty. You remember hearing something about a breakfast meeting for all the officials, so that must be where they are. And shouldn't you be with all the other girls pretending to eat breakfast right now?

Something in one of the rooms catches your eye. There, on a conference table, are several stacks of index cards, all carefully typed. You back up, making sure nobody's around, and then you can't help it, you move in. Typed in block letters are the words:

IF YOU COULD DO ONE THING TO HELP THE HOMELESS IN YOUR COMMUNITY, WHAT WOULD IT BE?

Oh shit. You glance at all the other cards. All questions. The interview questions. And each one has a little yellow Post-it with the name of a state on it. You're holding Alabama's card. But at the other end of the long table are the "V" states. Peeking would only take you a few seconds, and then you'd know the exact question they were going to ask you on national television. You could compose a response so poetic and heartbreaking, the world would weep.

Of course, it's kind of cheating—but unless you know the answer already, then it's not really cheating. It's sort of like when you're pretty sure you know the answer to part of a crossword puzzle but you just need to turn to the back page to check that you have the spelling right. That's not *cheating,* is it?

As your stoner ex-boyfriend once said, life will never give you answers if you don't know the right questions. At least you'll know yours by turning to page 109.

Come on, how hard will it be to answer Roddy's question about what kind of tree you'd be ("One with strong roots, Roddy"). Decide to wing it and walk away to page 116.

You are not going to deal with this aging pervert. His idea of a compromise probably involves getting you a pair of kneepads and a sash that says "Miss Congeniality."

"You know what," you say, struggling to free yourself from his grip, "I am going to try to forget that this ever happened, and burn the chilling scene from my brain."

"Hey, tiger," he says smoothly, "no need to get so feisty . . ."

"Don't sweet-talk me, grandpa." You turn to leave and say over your shoulder, "Good luck, California. Sure you'll *blow* the competition away." You run directly for the ladies' room, splash your face repeatedly with cold water, and consider vomiting in the toilet. Vomiting would be bad though—someone would undoubtedly assume you are bulimic and report you. Instead, you opt for an emergency cigarette on the backstage loading dock.

You have no idea what to do next. You are so disgusted that someone would trade sexual favors with a geriatric for the chance at the crown—that means what? The whole thing is just a silly game, not real life. And what are you going to do? Rush to the judges of said silly game and tell them that some-one is cheating? Who really cares? How did you, an honors student and star athlete, get into such a retarded situation?

On the other hand, you did not spend hours learning how to apply false eyelashes to have your dreams shattered by some little harlot with an oral fixation. Undecided, you return to the dressing room and begin shellacking pancake makeup on your face. You tell yourself the most important thing is to go out onstage focused and calm. If Miss California does indeed receive the crown and scepter, you can decide whether or not to blow the whistle on her later. It's showtime, and everyone you have ever befriended, slept with, pissed off, or shared a joint with is tuning in to see you.

You have not had a dream pageant, that's for sure. You were not paying attention during the opening number and almost tripped on a set piece, resulting in a body check by Miss Connecticut. One of the strings from your electric guitar snapped during the end of your talent performance, but hopefully the judges are not too familiar with Van Halen's "Hot for Teacher." You were so determined that everything go smoothly for the swimsuit competition that you overdid it with the adhesive spray and wound up removing a layer of delicate skin while taking off your bikini bottoms. You're trying to have a sense of humor about it, pretending it's a Brazilian gone awry.

But you know that it's a curse. The Curse of the Wrinkly Old Ass and the Cock-Sucking Californian. Ever since you laid eyes on that tableau, you have not been able to concentrate.

You are about to go onstage in your eveningwear and await the announcement of the five finalists when you feel a tap on your shoulder. You spin around to find yourself nose to nose with Miss Kneepads herself.

"Listen up, Burlington Coat Factory," Cali hisses, "open your mouth about this and you're going down."

"Funny," you reply, "since opening your mouth and going down seems to be one of your greatest talents."

She winds her manicured paw back and cracks you on the side of the face. You are caught reeling—it's not like you get bitch-slapped every day. Before you know it, you grab Cali by the back of her blonde updo and pull her down on her knees. She wails, but you could care less.

"Does this feel familiar?" you yell, shaking her head back and forth.

Suddenly, she swings her legs around and takes you out at the ankles, sending you to the floor. She is grabbing on to the straps of your gown, and the two of you are tangled and wrestling on the ground. Bobby pins whiz through the air, sequins fly, and lipstick is smeared. There is something visceral and satisfying about this kind of violence, you just didn't expect California to fight so dirty.

"*This is not Miss Liberty behavior!*" screams Fanny Mae Briar. She's like the referee in a boxing match, but nobody's listening.

California lands a catlike swipe across your face, the pain causing you to wince. Even she looks worried as you touch your cheek. When you look at your hand, it's spotted with red. That bitch has drawn blood! You stand up, dignified, looking to the gathering crowd for support. California wobbles to her feet, smoothing her hair and straightening her dress. You stare her down, face burning.

"Apologize!" barks Fanny Mae. You just turn to Miss California with a fake smile.

"Swallow this!" you growl, your hand forming a fist. You hit her in the face and the punch lands with a crack, like something from a movie. California drops like a rock.

Before you can say "disqualified" you are led away by hotel security. Miss California considers suing you, claiming you owe her future pageant earnings as well as an astronomical dental bill, but the suit is thrown out of court by a sensible judge who had trouble believing "pageanting" was a suitable career option. You, on the other hand, have been contacted by the Fox Network to participate in their next installment of *Celebrity Boxing*. You tell them yes, you will fight again, but only on the condition that you get to take on snot-nosed tennis diva Anna Kournikova. If negotiations go as planned, Anna's gonna get a taste of your backhand.

The End

You can't resist. The other girls would do it in a second. You walk to the end of the conference table and find the index card with the "Vermont" Post-it note.

"Oh goddammit . . ." you sigh. Your question reads: *"What would you do to resolve the crisis in the Middle East?"*

Now you're pissed. Elder statesmen, educated think tanks, and most presidents haven't been able to answer that question—so why would you of all people have the answer? You consider yourself extremely educated in international affairs. You even watch *Frontline* and have read one or two issues of *The Economist*! You quickly check the other girls' questions—they're all softball questions about their most insightful moment with children and how much they love their mothers. Why don't they give this whole Middle East question to that dumb-as-a-brick Miss Nebraska, who you overheard say that she thought if Princess Diana were still alive she could have won if she ran for president. You feel like you're going to pass out. This will be tough.

Remembering that you shouldn't be here, you race out of the room like it's on fire. It takes you a few tries to find the right elevator, but you get away scot-free. You have committed the perfect crime. You know your question and now you have to figure out the best way to answer it. The day ahead of you is pretty packed. You'll skip the stupid breakfast and the lunch—you'll be too nervous to eat anyway. If you show for the dress rehearsal, then skip the prayer circle, you'll have plenty of time to memorize your brilliant answer. You've got it all figured out. Now all you have to do is solve the crisis in the Middle East.

The lights are melting your makeup, Roddy Topper's teleprompter is just out of your peripheral vision, and the microphone is giving your voice a tinny echo. But you're totally composed. You're practically starting your answer before he finishes asking the question. You even do that cute crinkled-forehead "I'm really trying to think about this" expression that won you the Miss Burlington pageant. God, you're good.

"That's a difficult question, Roddy, but I'll try to answer it as best I can," you say. "If I were moderating between Israel and the Palestinians, I think I would begin by using the Oslo accords as a stepping stone. Now some may say that Oslo is irrelevant in today's cycle of violence, but I can't believe any peace agreement can be labeled irrelevant . . ." You continue on like you're Madeline Albright, throwing in phrases like *land for peace, intifada, Labor Party,* and *Wye accords*. You even drop in a few choice quotes from both sides of the argument. As you keep talking, the audience almost looks confused. How can you, beauty queen extraordinaire, have such a brilliant take on how to end a centuries-old conflict? How can you be so intelligent and still look like a babe in a swimsuit? they wonder. You're golden.

110

"Well, golly, that's quite a response," Roddy says, his mind blown.

"Thank you, Roddy," you say, with a humble nod.

When it comes down to the moment of truth, you're floating on air. Roddy has the envelope in his hands. Standing on stage with the four other finalists, you just can't picture any of them with the sash and crown. It's all you baby. When they announce the two finalists, you don't even blink. You know you're in there, baby, you're number one! Then the music swells and somebody hands Roddy that creamy envelope with your name inside it. You use your yoga skills to summon the tears of surprise you're going to need because he's tearing the envelope and he's saying . . .

"Miss Texas!"

You've got to be fucking kidding me. Miss Texas gasps and shakes, her knees buckling and her eyes welling with perfect tears—the kind that don't ruin the three-hour makeup job. You just stand there and applaud, trying to look grateful for the experience.

Backstage, you corner one of the pageant officials. Maybe it's the extra adrenaline or maybe it's the iron grip you have on her forearm, but she's a little more forthcoming than she ought to be.

"I'm sorry, but I heard they thought you just weren't accessible enough," she whispers, looking around for the exit.

"*Accessible* enough?" you hiss. "You mean I'm too *smart*!"

"They felt like America needed a Miss Liberty they could relate to on a more basic level."

"I'll take that as a compliment," you say.

The next day, you're standing in the lobby of your hotel, waiting for your family to pick you up. Life looks and feels a lot different when you're not wearing a pound of makeup. Scrubbed clean and dressed like a real person, you're kind of glad it's all over.

"Excuse me, are you Miss Vermont?" you hear from behind you. You turn around and nearly yelp—standing there are about five men and one woman, all looking intense and wearing muted suits. Clearly G-men.

"How can I help you?" you manage.

"We're from the U.S. State Department. We're here to offer you a job."

"Are you serious?"

"The secretary of state's children made her watch the Miss Liberty Pageant. We would like you to work with us on resolving the crisis in the Middle East."

You smile. "Well, it just so happens that I need a job."

The End

Since the day you got your Wonder Woman Underoos you have been a feminist at heart. You can't help but spread the good word.

"I think you girls have the wrong idea," you tell them. "Miss Liberty should be a role model for all women, whether they raise children or drive a forklift for a living."

"Omigod, only a dyke would drive a forklift," squeals Delaware.

"Okay," you say, your patience dwindling, "just take one piece of advice then. Tomorrow, push your tits out, smile big, and don't open your pathetic mouth."

"Omigod!" screams D.C., "I totally didn't realize—you're a dyke! God, that is so gross!"

You are frustrated, it's late, and you surrender. "Yes, honey. I am a big fat dyke. Big and gay as they come. And you better not piss me off or I will fondle you when you least expect it."

Just then, a taxicab pulls up and the girls pile in like they're being chased by a mugger. "You catch your own ride, lesbo," yells Miss Delaware out the window. Miss Nevada gives you an apologetic look as the cab pulls out onto the highway with your former state mates inside. You wander back through the parking lot to find a pay phone. As you sift through your purse looking for an emergency ciggie, you realize that you have absolutely no cash. You gave all your bills to the girls for the first cab ride—and now you are flat broke. That cheesy Ian guy may still be inside the bar, you think . . .

"Need a light?" You jump back and notice a man leaning up against a semi in the darkness. His face is shielded by a black cowboy hat, and his jeans are snug around his long legs and tight ass. Despite the huge belt buckle and the unfortunate Led Zeppelin T-shirt, you can tell this guy is one tall drink of water. You approach him warily. He probably has a pockmarked face and a mullet, you tell yourself.

"A light would be great," you say, holding up your cigarette. The lighter sparks and reveals a pair of twinkling blue eyes under thick eyebrows, chiseled cheekbones, and a mouth twisted into a sly grin. Not a pockmark in sight. You can't help but smile back.

"What's a pretty lady like you doing hanging out in a parking lot?" he asks.

"What's a cowboy doing in Reno?"

"Don't live here," he says, dragging on a hand-rolled cigarette, "just passing through." You detect a slight Texas accent that makes your knees soften. "I drive this here rig," he says, motioning to the semi.

"You're a trucker?" you ask. "I thought that all of you guys were fat old teamsters!"

"We are," he smiles, "I'm just not fat yet. Working on it though." He takes a long drag off his skinny cigarette and you catch a whiff of a familiar smell. Seeing that you've picked up on his joint, he asks, "Wanna hit?"

You have had a day from hell that started out with an 8 AM curtsey lesson, which morphed into a dance rehearsal complete with spirit fingers, and then a series of ridiculous interviews where you were forced to reveal how you really feel about important issues like self-esteem and body image. That is to say, you could definitely use a toke. And this handsome stranger may just be the answer to your prayers. He could get you high *and* drive you home—and as far as you're concerned, that makes him the perfect man.

Then again, would the perfect man be hanging out in a parking lot? And what if this weed is laced? Aren't truck drivers famous for transporting weed?

Take a hit and roll on home in a sixteen-wheeler by turning to page 119.

If you get high, you may do something dangerous like eat an entire large pizza the night before your swimsuit debut. Decline and turn to page 137.

In high school, you were the kind of girl who might cheat on her boyfriend but would never cheat on a test. Why change now? You'll be forever honest, no matter what. Even if it means looking like a moron on TV.

You are consoled to remember that the judges will inevitably pose some question about a platform. All the girls have a "platform," which is one of the few socially responsible parts of the Miss Liberty Pageant. Each girl chooses a social cause and learns everything there is to know about it. If crowned Miss Liberty, you are expected to use your media exposure to raise awareness for whatever cause you've chosen. The platforms in this year's pageant range from the standard to the bizarre. The most common seems to be the promotion of abstinence in schools, which the three bible-thumping girls have chosen, while only one girl (Massachusetts, bless her heart) has chosen to promote sex education in schools. Both Rhode Island and Kansas are fighting to raise awareness for asthma sufferers and you've heard that Miss Louisiana has taken up the cause of those poor racing greyhounds that get sent to the death chamber when they can't race anymore. Now *that's* a platform.

You tried a few different causes, things you really care about, but censorship was too broad and medical marijuana was never a plausible possibility. You finally chose a platform that made sense to you and the fair state of Vermont—

convincing local dairy farmers to donate some of their live-stock to send to impoverished villages in Africa. One cow or goat can change a family's entire future by providing milk to drink and sell. What means so little to a Vermont dairy farm can mean so much to a family halfway around the world. You're so lost in thought, you don't notice you're not alone anymore.

"Miss Vermont, I presume?" a voice with a cheesy French accent asks. It's Réné, the thick, balding guy from Montréal who can't get over the whole French-Canadian issue. He may not be from our great nation, but he *is* the token diversity judge, about as exotic as you can get and still relatively English-speaking. You should have smelled him before you'd seen him. His musk cologne must actually come from muskrats. It's foul.

"Is this the ladies' room?" you try.

"Zis is quite a violation, I sink," he says. He's coming closer to you. Wait—he's coming *on* to you!

"Interesting you should use the term 'violate' because—" ugh! He's stroking your arm! "I didn't look at the questions and I don't think you should immediately assume I would."

"You know somesinck?" Réné says, pawing you, "I can make zis all go away. I can help you. But being a judge for Miss Liberty has made me so tense, I feel I need . . . some *release.*" You try not to throw up as he nuzzles you with his half-stubbled, musky face.

How important is this pageant to you? Réné's holding all the cards whether or not you looked at yours. Reject his nasty advances and it's surely over for you. But to give in would be . . . well, it'd be gross, not to mention traumatic—but it may be the only way to win.

Give Réné his release. Nobody's going to know if you pretend it never happened. The crown might be waiting for you on page 123.

Fondling the French Canadian is not on your list of things you'd do to win the Miss Liberty Pageant. Keep your dignity by going to page 129.

Take a toke and relax! Your year of pageant hell is almost over!

You take a drag of his joint and smile. It has been more than a year since you got high, due to the barrage of drug tests the pageant police administer. But your year of abstinence is nearly over! Actually, it *is* over! Everyone will be so crazed tomorrow, there is no way they are going to put the girls through testing again. . . .

You and your trucker friend smoke up and talk Van Halen. He is really impressed to hear you can play almost every one of their guitar solos. You both ponder why the David Lee Roth years are so far superior to the Sammy Haggar era. Basically, you talk about the really important things in life.

"Look," you say, "I know you drive all day, so this may be a pain in your ass. But can you give me a ride? I need to get back home."

Truckerman escorts you to the passenger-side door and literally lifts you off your feet and places you inside. As you hurtle through the darkness toward the glow of downtown Reno, he lets you play with the two-way radio and pull on the cord that honks the big horn. You do feel a bit conspicuous being dropped at the casino entrance in a semi, though.

He scribbles something on a half-used pack of Lucky Strikes and tosses them to you as you leave. As the truck creeps off in the distance, you glance down at the pack in your hands and giggle. It's a name, number, and a website that reads: www.hottruckerguys.com. Your baby is a center-fold.

You carefully apply fake eyelashes in front of your vanity mirror backstage. It's one hour to showtime and you've never felt better. With a little herbal assistance, you slept like a baby last night. All the other girls are yawning and trying to cover the bags under their eyes as a result of their restless evening. Not you.

"Vermont! Got something for you." You spin around. Her name is Fanny Mae Briar, whose sweet-sounding Southern name doesn't fool you. She is the head of the Miss Liberty Pageant—the queen bee. The only thing more frightening than her nest of white blonde hair and her affinity for fuchsia suits is her passion for etiquette and morality amongst "her girls."

She hands you a plastic cup with a label that reads "Vermont." Your stomach drops as you realize that you have underestimated the thoroughness of the pageant Gestapo. "This is standard procedure and administered completely at random," she says with a plastic smile. Seeing your face, she asks, "Is there a problem honey?"

"No," you stammer. "It's just that I put on my pantyhose already, and my leotard, and . . ." you look up and realize that you are not going to elicit any sympathy from this old bird. She hands you the cup and tells you that you have five minutes, then walks off.

"Fuck, what a bummer." You look over to see Miss Nevada, your next-mirror neighbor. She regards you with pity, "A drug test an hour before curtain? That's just fucking wrong."

"Well if you guys hadn't abandoned me last night, I wouldn't have been forced to catch a ride home with a pot-smoking trucker."

"Jesus," she says, "I am really sorry about that. Those small-state bitches must have gotten to me. Let me make it up to you."

"How?" you ask cautiously.

"Do you want some of my piss?" she asks, without taking her eyes off her reflection.

Using her pee sounds like a brilliant plan, but there are many potential pitfalls. For instance, do you know if you can trust Nevada to keep quiet and not squeal to the officials? She *is* morally bankrupt, after all. And if you get caught in the bait-and-switch, it's possible the pageant police can call the real police, and then you will be forced to sit through twelve weeks of rehab meetings in a smoke-filled room in a church basement. You shudder at the thought.

Besides, you read somewhere that you need to smoke an insane amount of dope to have it show up in a test. And what drug lab could they possibly have on the premises? By the time everything is announced, and you are crowned Miss Liberty, who cares about the test? They won't want a scandal, after all. They're the ones who let the dope-smoking likes of you into their pageant.

Buying piss is about as shameful as buying a Pabst Blue Ribbon, and you've done that before. Buy a pot o' gold and turn to page 126.

You are not a fuck-up parolee! You are a beauty queen! And you are going to pee in your own damn cup! Turn to page 132.

Just try to think of all the good that will come from this nasti-ness. You never have to see Réné again, you never have to think about it again, it can't be any more gross than when the family dog had that digestion problem. . . .

"What do I need to do?" you ask Réné, near tears.

"You zink me a monster," he says, unbuttoning his shirt. You shake your head "no" but your expression obviously means, "yes, you creepy bastard." He takes your hands and puts them on his clammy, fatty chest. "You know the art of massage, yes?"

"I guess."

"I'm going to lie down zere on zhat sofa, and you are going to give me a massage."

"That's all?" you ask, trying not to sound hopeful.

"And I want you to take off all of your clothes."

"Huh?"

"Nothink relaxes me more zhan a massage from a beauti-ful naked woman forty years my junior. Zee hotel was not as accommodatink as you will be."

"But we don't have to have sex, right?"

"No! I am a married man and very religious. But I have my needs. And a naked massage from you, I need very much."

"And if I do this for you, what are you going to do for me?"

"If you can loosen zee knot of nerves in my neck, you will wear zee crown tonight. I have all zee judges wrapped around my finger."

123

Okay, this isn't as bad as you thought, but it's still pretty bad. Réné strips down to his shorts and plops down on the sofa. It takes you a while to get up the courage to get naked, but you steel your resolve and do it. Réné gives you a long, lascivious look, but he's true to his word—he doesn't touch you. You, however, have to touch his gross, musky skin. You knead away at his back and neck and arms, taking out all your pain and embarrassment on him. Réné moans, faster and harder as you continue to drive your fists into his back. You're welling up with tears, naked and embarrassed, sick from the putrid stink.

"*Ahhh . . . Yesssss!*" Réné groans, guttural and phlegmy. You step back, horrified. Réné has gotten his release. You quickly pull your clothes on, ashamed. As you head out the door, you hear his voice one more time: "Zank you, Miss Liberty."

"Miss Vermont, our new Miss Liberty!" Roddy shouts. The other girls on the stage with you scream and cry, hugging and congratulating you. Last year's Miss Liberty gives up her crown and passes it to you as you stand there, completely unemotional. That is, until you see Réné in the judge's box, applauding. And then you start to cry.

A few weeks later, *The New York Times* prints a scathing exposé of the Miss Liberty judging scandal. It turns out that you won only because a certain French Canadian judge gave you exceptionally high scores, even when they weren't merited. Miss Texas and your old roomie, Miss Florida, are part of a group of girls suing the Miss Liberty organization. Rumors are flying about sexual favors and late-night payments. You've denied everything, of course, but your reign as Miss Liberty has been tainted by this scandal. They've even asked you to consider stepping down like that one beauty queen who showed up in *Penthouse.*

You watch CNN as Réné, a.k.a. the embattled Miss Liberty judge, prepares to make a statement to the press. Flash-bulbs go off and reporters quiet down as he clears his throat. He points a thick finger at the media.

"I did not have . . . sexual relations with zhat woman, Miss Vermont . . ."

Well, you think, he *is* right. Of course that depends on what your definition of "is" is.

The End

You have possessed a few shameful items in your day: drugs, sex toys, and the occasional boy band CD. But you're proud to say you've never needed anyone's piss but your own—until now.

"Um, would you really mind?" you inquire timidly. "You would really be helping me out . . ."

"No sweat, sweetie," Nevada says. She tows you off to the ladies' room, plastic cup in hand. The bathroom is packed, but Nevada grabs you by the wrist and pulls you into the large handicapped stall at the end of the row.

"Hey, Vermont, I need your help taping my thong into place!" she yells for the benefit of any potential eavesdroppers. She grabs the cup out of your hands and hikes up her sequined miniskirt, decorated to look like the Las Vegas Strip. You politely try to avert your eyes as she squats over your cup and fills it up. As she twists a plastic cap on the newly filled testing cup, she says, "Hey, how about after this dog and pony show is over, we hit the town. I would sell my soul for a dirty martini."

"Yes," you agree, "very dirty."

You hurriedly hand off "your" urine sample to old lady Fanny Mae, touch up your chipping toenails, spray your orange-hued nylons with hairspray to prevent snags, and cover up what you only wish was a hickey but is probably a rash from that cowbell choker they make you wear in the opening number.

Showtime hits, and you enter the stage with a giant cardboard cutout of the state of Vermont in your hands and a dairy-themed headdress all but stapled to your head. Your opening number goes off without a hitch. And when you are called to the microphone to give your name and state, what you are really thinking is: "Hello. My name is *badass, dope smoking, urine swapping rebel,* and I am representing the great state of Vermont!" You always heard that you should smile like you have a secret. Well, honey, you have one.

You are backstage, changing into your first evening gown of the night for the "lineup," the part of the show where all fifty women are paraded onstage, from which ten are selected to compete in the final categories.

While you're struggling with a sandal strap, Miss Ohio skips up to you. "I hear congratulations are in order," she whispers. She trots off with a wink before you can ask her what she knows. You stand up and take a deep breath. Adrenaline shoots through you. You must be one of the ten finalists! How does she know so early? You look around to see little groups of women whispering and looking over toward you curiously.

You are in the wings waiting to enter the stage when Miss Iowa, one of the favorites to win, shimmies up next to you and squeezes your shoulder. "Congrats, Vermont. Who would have thought?" She is looking at you with palpable contempt, but you are sure it's jealousy. You know you will beat her if you land in the top ten. She has an "athletic" figure and belts out Broadway tunes, while you have a "voluptuous" figure and play metal guitar.

Just as the music cues up, you spot Fanny Mae out of the corner of your eye, and she's motioning you over. You figure she is probably going to apologize for making you, one of the top contestants, take a drug test backstage. "We need to talk," she says, in a mothering tone. She is about to dispel a nugget of pageant wisdom, and you smile and wait.

"Your tests came back negative for drug use," she begins. You cover your mouth to hide your audible sigh of relief. "However, it does show that you are *expecting*." She says the word "expecting" in hushed and embarrassed tones, like she's saying the word "vagina."

"Expecting what?"

Fanny Mae notices your blank look and says with tears of joy in her eyes, "You're pregnant! You are going to be a mommy!" You have a momentary panic attack, then you remember you haven't had sex in two months! Unless this kid's the second coming, there must be some mistake. Then you realize *you're* not pregnant at all—Miss Nevada is! "Of course," Fanny Mae continues, "we expect you will be keeping the child, and we cannot allow Miss Vermont to be a single mother . . ."

You realize that this is the end of the road. You may not have tested positive for drugs, but you're still out, and you're not about to get yourself busted for the urine swap. You touch your belly and try to fake a beatific and nurturing smile. "Thank you, Fanny," you swoon. "Thank you for this wonderful news." You gather your things backstage and head directly to the casino lounge. You deserve a glass of champagne or two to celebrate. Okay, so you're not Miss Liberty, but at least you're not knocked up.

The End

There's no way in hell you're going to wrestle with Réné. You have a certain amount of dignity left and you plan to keep it.

"You know, I've spent the last year convincing my friends and family that Miss Liberty is not degrading to women. Because I never really truly felt degraded. Until right now."

"I did not mean to suggest . . ." Réné fumbles, stepping away.

"Oh yes you did. I came into this room looking for a bathroom; there is no way I would even consider compromising my strong moral fiber by looking at my interview question. That you would even suggest such a thing just makes me sick. And you're supposed to be here representing our neighbors from the north? What would the people of Canada think if they knew what you just suggested?" You get closer to him, summon up a tear. "What would the *French* Canadians think?"

Réné, chastened, takes a seat. He looks up at you, full of regret. "I am zo zorry . . ."

At that moment, the door swings open. It's Fanny Mae Briar, Miss Liberty 1963. She's the president of the Miss Liberty Foundation and feared by men and women alike. "What in heaven's name is going on in here?"

"This . . . *creep* was trying to get me to perform sexual favors."

"What?!" Fanny exclaims, nearly having a seizure.

"I wandered into this room by mistake and he *cornered* me," you say, trying to look wounded. "I think I need to go. My best friend from college who works at the *Washington Post* is supposed to meet me for an interview about my pageant experiences. I really can't be late." Okay, that part isn't true, but you do have a friend from college who works as an assistant at the *Post*. His ambition is to be either Woodward or Bernstein so he's definitely looking for a big story to break his career.

"Oh . . . oh . . . *look*," Fanny Mae says in a between-you-and-me way. "We don't want this little incident to taint your Miss Liberty experience."

"It's definitely tainted," you say, glaring at Réné.

"What if we made you an offer?"

"What, hush money?"

"We certainly couldn't let you compete in the competition at this point. We can't get another judge and it wouldn't be right for Réné to score you up or down because of this incident."

"But I'm here to compete," you explain.

"I understand. There's nothing quite like being on that stage, representing your state, and going for the crown, but I don't see how we can allow you to continue."

"But you think you can shut me up."

"The prize is twenty thousand dollars. We're prepared to offer you that much, aren't we, Réné?"

"No more sailboat down-payment," Réné says with hound dog eyes.

"Twenty-five," you counter.

"Nice try," Fanny Mae shoots back.

"Twenty-five or I go to my friend and spill every gory detail. Miss Liberty will be finished and so will you."

"Allright," Fanny Mae sighs. "Twenty-five thousand. But on one condition: you drop out of the pageant right here and now."

"Then again, there's a chance I could win the whole thing. I could tell the world all about my platform and really do some good as Miss Liberty. What if I want to keep going?"

"Then it's your word against ours, right Réné?" Fanny says, kicking Réné.

"Whatever you say, Fanny," he says.

Fanny puts on her beauty-queen smile. "So what'll it be?"

Fanny's offer is pretty tempting, considering you have no guarantee you'll win Miss Liberty. Take the twenty-five grand and make a grand exit on page 135.

Americans never got anywhere bargaining with the French or the Canadians, so turn to page 139.

Swapping piss is about as glamorous as smuggling drugs in your ass. You are going to do the dignified thing: panic.

"I'll manage," you tell Nevada and your own reflection. "I will be just fine."

You try to tweeze any microscopic stray eyebrow hairs, but your hands are shaking so much, you are in danger of poking out an eye. You feel a familiar and awful sensation in your stomach—the same feeling you got when you were sent to the principal's office in second grade, or the time you got caught shoplifting lip-gloss when you were thirteen. It's the worst of all fears: the fear of getting caught.

"Vermont!" A familiar shriek jolts you. "Chop, chop! Two minutes!" In the reflection you can see perky Fanny Mae gesticulating toward an imaginary watch. You grab your purse and the empty cup and bolt. You make your way through the labyrinth backstage. You don't know exactly where you are going, but you need to escape. It's like you are in the crosshairs of some assassin up in a bell tower.

Hindus meditate, Catholics pray, and you smoke. You will smoke a cigarette and then decide what to do. You rush out onto the casino floor, safe from prying eyes of backstabbing contestants and the pageant police. Sparking up a cigarette, you circle the floor. You watch the throngs of humanity coursing through the casino—the tourists throwing away their children's college funds, the fratboys enjoying their morning beers, your parents. . . . Your parents!!! Sure enough, there are Mom and Dad, both wearing Vermont T-shirts, across the crowded floor.

You spin around to face a wall of slot machines, silently praying Mom and Pops didn't spot you. How would you explain not being backstage, never mind the fact that you are smoking cigarettes again? You huddle down in the biggest chair you can find, in front of a high-roller slot machine that costs five dollars a pull. You snort at the thought. Who plays five-dollar slots?

"Excuse me, Miss?" An old lady with a shock-orange Afro and a floral casino-issue vest is hovering over you. "You are not allowed to be in this area unless you are playing the machine."

"Okay," you mutter, pulling out your last twenty-dollar bill. She hands you four gold coins, and you drop one into the slot. Just as you are wondering if your parents are safely out of your path, the machine starts whirling, buzzing, and beeping. A siren goes off over your head, and the old lady who changed your twenty rushes toward you! Unbelievably, you have won!!! You are in such shock, you cannot comprehend how much you are collecting—the digital counter continues to climb to higher and higher numbers. . . .

After a barrage of security guards checked your identification, date of birth, and social security number, you were cut a check for $1.2 million. The hotel kindly put you and your parents up for the evening in the high-roller suite complete with indoor swimming pool, rotating bed, and a twenty-four-hour butler service. Okay, you may not have won the Miss Liberty Pageant, but you are Reno's newest millionaire. Now you have more liberty than you've ever dreamed of.

The End

A great man once said, "You have to know when to hold 'em, know when to fold 'em, know when to walk away, and know when to run." You're taking the cash consolation prize.

"Deal. I get the twenty-five G's and you get my resignation."

"Yes. I think you've come down with a terrible cold," Fanny says with a thin smile. "Would you join me downstairs? Casino chips are the best way to handle this."

"Untraceable. Huh. Fanny, your momma didn't raise no fool." You turn to René, who is now making unhappy snorting noises, clearly distressed he has to pay up. "Au revoir," you say with a smirk.

You and Fanny soon find your way downstairs to the massive casino. Fanny steps up to the casino cage, gets the manager, and has no problem getting twenty-five gold thousand-dollar chips. They're heavy and cold and beautiful.

"I'd wait a while, cash them in, and run home to Vermont as fast as your Birkenstocks will carry you," Fanny purrs.

"It's been a pleasure," you say, and kiss her on both cheeks, *Godfather* style.

You find the closest bar and order up a double Ketel One on the rocks. As you drain it down, the only regret you have is for your platform. You decide you'll give ten G's to the cause, and keep fifteen to pay back all those bills you've racked up getting here. The dresses, the shoes—everything has really taken a bite. You order another drink.

You're on your way out of the casino, a little tipsy from the double vodkas, when you see the high-rollers' roulette table. Fuck your credit cards. Without so much as a second thought, you put fifteen one-thousand-dollar chips on number twenty-five. You figure you just stumbled onto the cash, so why not? The croupier at the wheel calls his pit boss over, makes sure you're sure, and spins the wheel. You're only slightly nervous as the wheel slows. And slows. And that tick-tick-tick of the ball. People are gathering to watch. You almost reach for your bet but know it's too late.

"Twenty-five!" shouts the croupier. A cheer goes up. You can't focus for a moment, and then you realize you just won a shitload of money.

A year later, you're in Uganda at a ribbon-cutting ceremony, standing next to Bono and Angelina Jolie. You've just opened up a nonprofit agricultural school. Hundreds of teenagers and adults are going to learn the skills to survive and prosper off the land. A whole community will see their children grow up with a better economic environment because you entered a beauty pageant, took a payoff, and drank too much vodka on an empty stomach. Life's funny that way.

The End

*You've managed to stay relatively clean and sober for a year.
Twenty-four more hours sans purple haze isn't going to kill
you. . . .*

"Under any other circumstances, I would take you up on
that offer," you tell the handsome trucker. "I just can't
smoke tonight."

"Why?" he chuckles. "You out on parole? Drive school
buses for a living? In the Miss Liberty Pageant?"

"How did you know?" you ask in shock.

He laughs. "It was a lucky guess. I've got a truckload of set
pieces for the show tomorrow." He takes another drag.
"You're sure pretty enough to be a beauty queen." You blush
in the darkness.

"So how is the life of a trucker treating you?" you ask, then
immediately curse yourself for saying something so lame.

"It's rough," he begins, "it's lonely, the hours are long, and
it's dangerous. You have no idea how many times I've been
held up and ripped off. The worst part is, we're invisible to
most of the country, and those who see us think we're scum."

Suddenly, your trucker seems like he's just a lost little
boy—a lost little boy you wanna make out with. "I'm so
sorry. I don't think you're scummy at all." You touch his
cheek and say, "Look, I'm sure pretty girls ask you this all the
time, but will you give me a ride home in your truck? I'm supposed to be tucked in by now for the show tomorrow—"

You stop talking because suddenly you're blinded by a bright white light. You blink, trying to see where it's coming from, but your trucker fills in the blanks for you.

"Shit. The fuzz," he exclaims, tossing down his joint.

The light goes out and you see the cops heading for you, sirens blaring and lights on. Your body breaks out in a cold sweat. There are clearly drugs present—if you get arrested you're screwed.

"What do we do?"

"We either run or we hide."

"What?"

"There's a place we can take cover—it's not far from here—but we gotta make a run for it," he says quickly.

"Run for it? How far?"

He shrugs, unsure. Then he glances at the rows and rows of big rig trucks. "Or if we're real crafty we can take our chances here and hide. My buddy's rig's not far."

If you'd rather hide in some trucker's cab and hope the cops don't smoke you out, turn to page 149.

Just because you run doesn't mean they'll chase you. If you're willing to take that chance, head for the hideout on page 143.

You will not be a kept woman! You've come this far and now you know you cannot be bought for any price!

"You can take your weak-ass offer and shove it," you tell Fanny.

"Well I *never*!" she exclaims.

"Yeah, bet you've never," you shoot back, breezing past her. You give Réné one last what-would-your-mother-say look and then you're out of there.

"You report this and we'll just see what happens!" screams Fanny. "You don't know who you're dealing with!"

In between dress rehearsals, you're frantically trying to get your defense ready. You've left five messages for your friend who works at the *Post*, but as it turns out, he went to Amsterdam a month ago and never returned. He always was a pothead first and an idealist reporter second. When you get to the theater for the show, you're surprised to find your dressing area has been cleaned out.

"What's going on?" you ask Miss Texas.

"Don't ask me, darlin'.' They came and got your things about twenty minutes ago. They told me to tell you to go to the green room."

Great. You knew you should have gone to the pageant officials first, then the press. It would have made a better story, too, the officials ignoring your pleas for help, the media being the only place you could turn. . . . You curse yourself as you head for the green room. Opening the door, you find a strange sight: your parents.

"Mom? Dad? I thought I wasn't allowed to see you guys until after the pageant was over!"

"Well, they made an exception," says your father, giving you a weak embrace. Your mom stays in her seat, crying.

"Mom—are you okay?" you ask.

"If you were having such problems, I wish you would have told us!" she cries.

"Problems?" you ask, confused. When you turn around, you realize there is a team of large burly men in jumpsuits behind you. A severe looking man wearing glasses approaches you carefully. He looks like a doctor of some sort.

"You're going to take a rest now," he says, the men moving in toward you.

"What is this—who are you people?" you ask, knowing exactly who they are. They all seem to think you've gone Mariah or something. "If Fanny told you to come and get me, this is all a big misunderstanding. That judge Réné tried to sleep with me and Fanny made all these threats . . ."

"Come on now, honey, you know that's not true," says your mother, weeping.

"We know the kind of pressure this type of competition can put a girl under. But what's most important is your health. Your mental health," your father says.

"Yes, it iz for zee best," grumbles a familiar voice. Réné! He waltzes into the room with Fanny Mae Briar on his arm, trying to look concerned.

"You French Canadian muskrat!" you shout. You look to

your parents, pleading. "Come *on*! You can't trust the Canadians and you can't trust the French! He's the sick one, not me!"

"You see what I mean?" Fanny purrs.

"I'm not crazy," you say rationally, trying another tack.

"We're taking you to a safe place," the doctor says.

"What? A place where I get to make crafts out of dry macaroni and pipe cleaners? Where lights out is at nine o'clock? I can't do that institutional food shit—are you sure you don't want to take my roommate, Miss Child Pageant Florida? She's nuts! I'm perfectly normal!"

Your pleas fall on deaf ears. The last thing you see is a massive hypodermic needle heading for your thigh. That's going to leave a mark for the swimsuit competition, for sure.

When you wake up, you're in a dusty chair that smells like vomit. Patients in white, loose-fitting gowns shuffle all around you. You look down at your clothes. You're dressed the same way. You wipe the drool from your mouth and try to focus. It's pretty clear you're in the rec-room of the psycho ward. It's like something out of *Twelve Monkeys,* only there's no Brad Pitt.

Somewhere in the back of your head, you can hear the drone of a television.

"Turn that up," you mumble. Nobody responds. They're all on too many barbiturates. "Turn it up!" you shout.

Some manic guy grabs the remote and starts dancing around, cranking up the volume as loud as it will go. Roddy

Topper is on the screen, tearing open an envelope. It's a news clip of last night's Miss Liberty Pageant.

". . . Miss Florida!" he says, beaming. Your roommate bursts into tears, the music swelling. You stand up and walk to the television in disbelief as she's crowned Miss Liberty. When it comes time to speak, she looks right into the camera.

"This goes out to my roommate, who taught me what was important. My conversation with her changed my life, and now, I'm Miss Liberty! This is for you, Vermont! I know you'll get healthy soon!"

Great. Your crazy roommate is Miss Liberty and it's all because of your careful guidance. After a moment of suppressed rage, you return to your chair and chase some twitchy guy out of it by telling him there's an elf hiding behind the nurses' station.

"So," you ask nobody in particular, "what's a girl gotta do to get a Vicodin around here?"

The End

You haven't run from the cops since you got busted TP-ing your seventh grade teacher's house! Those were the days—and here you are again! Run!

Your trucker grabs you by the wrist and pulls you through rows and rows of semis lining the parking lot. You can hear the wail of the police siren behind you, as the police spotlight chases you. You zig and zag back and forth, trying to lose the cops. Suddenly there is a thunderous sound of one of the trucks' roll-doors opening. You are yanked by the scruff of your neck into the back of the truck, and the door slams shut with a bang.

It is pitch dark inside the truck, and it takes a few moments for your eyes to adjust. You feel the hand of your trucker resting on your thigh. And you can make out the forms of several other men sitting next to you. You turn to your new trucker boyfriend, and he signals to be quiet. Outside, you hear the police roll by several times before they give up the search, gun the engine, and peel out onto the highway.

A match sparks up the truck, and you find yourself with half a dozen truckers sitting on boxes around a makeshift table full of money and cards. Your guy stands up and starts high-fiving and backslapping the other men.

"You old son of a bitch," an older man is saying, "I told you to lay off that reefer, man!"

"I know, I know," your trucker says. He motions to you,

"Gentlemen, I want you to meet the love of my life and my future ex-wife, Miss Vermont!"

You smile at the truckers. "Thank you so much for rescuing us," you say. "I don't think the Miss Liberty Pageant would look too kindly on one of their own winding up in prison."

"No problemo, beautiful," one of the older truckers says. "You can be here on one condition. You have to shoot whiskey and play cards."

You sit down at the table, and they deal you in. You tell the men you don't want their money, but you do need a ride back to the casino strip. Several hands of hold-em later, the truckers owe you so many rides you could make it to Mexico and back.

"Don't worry about paying me back," you joke, as you leave the truck. "Just tell your teamster friends to fix it so that I win tomorrow." The men nod as you walk toward your trucker's semi for your ride home.

The next day, a miracle happens. You make it to the final five. It's overwhelming as you stand next to the four other finalists, awaiting your final interview question. You have to admit, your opening number was a less than exemplary performance. You tangled your legs in the cow tail of your dairy-themed Vermont costume and you nearly took Miss Connecticut out at the kick line. The swimsuit competition felt a little off, too—but who feels comfortable prancing around in a bikini and Lucite heels? The best part of the pageant was definitely your talent performance—okay, the outfit you got to wear for the talent performance. All the other girls were so jealous of the custom flame-stitched leather pants and sparkly rocker T-shirt you wore while performing Van Halen's "Hot for Teacher" on electric guitar.

The emcee, Roddy Topper, is working his way down to you with the final question. You gaze out into the audience, flashing your glittering smile. You're not sure if you're seeing things, but it looks like your trucker stud is in one of the first rows. And he appears to be surrounded by dozens of other similarly disheveled looking teamsters. Your mind might be playing tricks on you—after all, they could be Miss Tennessee's brothers and uncles or something.

"Miss Vermont," Roddy Topper says, snapping you out of your daze, "who would you say are the unsung heroes of America?" You look out into the dim crowd, and you have an epiphany. There is a reason you have advanced this far, and it has nothing to do with your charm, poise, and talent: You have the teamsters behind you. In a flash you change your mind about delivering that love letter of a speech to all the public-school teachers in America.

"Well, Roddy, what makes this country so dynamic is our thriving free-market economy. And most Americans don't know that most of our products travel across the country on wheels. The men and women who guide these trucks through the open landscape of our beautiful nation truly move America. They safeguard our economy and make this nation work. I believe that truck drivers are the backbone of our nation, the true American heroes. Thank you." Wild applause erupts from a certain section of the audience, while the rest of the theater is in silent shock.

Ten minutes and a commercial break later Roddy has an envelope in his hand that will reveal the next Miss Liberty. You are waiting for your name to be read as fourth or third or second runner-up, but those honors have gone to Miss Utah, Miss Oregon, and Miss South Carolina. You are one of two women left. You look over to Miss Texas, your only opponent, and smile. "Kiss my ass, tree hugger," she hisses under her breath.

"And the first runner-up is, Miss Texas!"

An adrenaline rush courses through you as you realize you are Miss Liberty! You never thought you would care about winning this damn thing, but God, this feels amazing. You try not to hyperventilate as they place the crown on your head, scepter in your hand, and sash over your shoulder. You have the vague notion that tonight you will celebrate with a bottle of pink champagne and a very handsome trucker.

Word spreads quickly among the truckers of America. As you're spending your year doing the required traveling and charity work, your story grows and changes. By the time you've handed over the crown to the next year's Miss Liberty, you've become a trucker folk hero. After signing a few licensing agreements, your image has begun to pop up on mudflaps, calendars, and T-shirts. It's even common for truckers to have your swimsuit-competition photo airbrushed onto the sides of their semi rigs. You're only Miss Liberty for a year, but your face will drive trucks across our great country for years to come.

The End

Miss Florida obviously has issues no mere beauty queen can cure. She needs a team of shrinks from Switzerland. You'd much rather bond with the sane chicks down the hall.

Worried that Miss Florida might crack, you wait until she goes to the bathroom and race out of your room like it's on fire. Out of breath, you knock on Miss Montana's door. The second you're inside you feel better.

"Oh my *God*, you would not believe what just happened," you say, demanding their attention. "I just found out my roommate is totally JonBenet Ramsey. Kid pageants, the whole bit." You wait for the horrified reactions.

"What's wrong with child pageants?" one of them asks. And it's a genuine question. You smile and change the subject.

"So, what are we all doing tonight?"

"Truth or dare," says Miss Montana.

"Wow. Tres summer camp."

"Tell me about it. That's why it's so neat! And it's a way to get to know one another better."

You've kept your distance from these girls, because you don't believe in getting too close to the competition. But maybe that's only an excuse. All these girls seem perfectly nice, but you have to admit they aren't people you would hang with back home. In fact, hiding behind those perfect smiles are some of the biggest nerds you have ever met. You doubt any of these girls could open a beer with their teeth or make a bong out of a McDonald's Happy Meal toy, like your friends at home have been known to do. But maybe you shouldn't judge . . .

"Truth or dare sounds great," you say with a smile.

"I just *knew* you were loads of fun!" shrieks Miss Montana, hugging you frantically. You try to respond with equal enthusiasm, but it's medically impossible.

"Okay," says Miss Missouri. "So what will it be? Truth or dare?"

"It's my turn?"

"New girls go first!" exclaims the ever-excited Miss Louisiana.

"Okay," you agree. It's their party; you play by their rules.

They say it shall set you free. If you think truth is your best bet, turn to page 166.

Taking a dare is how you wound up at Miss Liberty in the first place! Show these girls how it's done and pick dare by going to page 152.

Running's so undignified. However, hiding like a scared little girl works for you. . . .

Your hot trucker grabs your hand and yanks you down, pressing you against the asphalt and rolling you behind the wheels of a semi.

"Do not try to hide . . ." say the cops on their bullhorn. "You're only making things worse . . ."

A beam of light sweeps near your feet and your trucker takes off, worm-style, and you follow him like you're on an army obstacle course. Seconds later you're at the foot of a metallic blue cab. He stands, eases the door open, and motions for you to get inside. You leap in and he's right behind you. He shuts the door just as the cop car cruises past.

"Are we safe?" you ask, eyes adjusting.

"Sure thing, babe," he says with a grin. "Just keep your head down and we'll be safe. This is my buddy's cab. We can stay here as long as we want."

Your eyes adjust to your surroundings. The walls are covered with cheesy porno cutouts. This guy is definitely a breast man. You start laughing, and so does your hot trucker friend. Pretty soon he's whispering trucker stories to you and you're near tears laughing. You lose track of time, and it seems like the cop car has stopped its drive-bys.

"This has been a wild night," you say, inching closer to him. You're not getting out of the cab without kissing him. You're moments away from that lofty goal when the cab fills with light. "What is this, an alien abduction?" you say, freaking.

But it's no UFO, it's a helicopter. One of many. The place is teeming with police. The cops left and brought back reinforcements.

"Bail out, sugar!" the trucker shouts, throwing open the door and making a break for it. You both bolt toward the trees without being spotted. By the time you stop running, you're in a little hillside clearing, looking down at the parking lot below. It looks like something out of a movie, dozens of cop cars, helicopters, and vans.

You hear some guy on a loudspeaker shouting "Impound them all. Every single one!"

You can tell by the look on your trucker's face that this is bad news. He sinks to a squat, defeated. "My ass is grass," he says. "And so's yours, Miss Vermont." Wait . . . didn't he mention something about transporting set pieces for the Miss Liberty Pageant? "Your pretty little pageant's in impound."

You managed to sweet-talk a sheriff into dropping you off at the hotel just hours before the pageant begins. It's now thirty minutes to curtain, and everything is a fucking disaster. Pageant officials are running around screaming like banshees. Apparently, they cannot locate a giant moving staircase, an integral pageant set piece; instead, a huge cross was delivered to the theater. The giant glittery rainbow-colored backdrop of Miss Liberty that is supposed to hang onstage has been replaced at the last moment by a barren desert landscape scene. And the red, white, and blue sparkly leotards that all the contestants are supposed to wear for a patriotic dance number are missing—in their place are heaps of burlap togas.

After the show is postponed indefinitely, it is discovered that the Miss Liberty set and props have been "accidentally" impounded, and the only sets available were those borrowed at the last minute from the national touring company of *Jesus Christ Superstar*. At least you can claim your Miss Liberty Pageant was a religious experience.

The End

There's nothing these girls could think up that you wouldn't do. You dare them to embarrass you!

"Dare."

"Nobody chooses dare!"

"I do."

"Oh mah gawd! I knew you Vermont girls were crazy!" screams Miss Louisiana.

"Well, all we have out there are two months of warm weather and lots of free time," you say. She doesn't know the half of it.

"We haven't thought up a dare yet," says Miss Montana, nose crinkled with utter confusion. "Secret circle!" she squeals. All the girls seem to understand exactly what she means. It's like they've got their own language.

All of the girls gather in the far corner of the room, giggling and coming up with ideas about what your dare is going to be. You're getting bored, but every so often one of the girls will gasp or start screaming and you know they're giving it *way* too much thought. Just as you're about to make an excuse and leave, they scamper back to you.

"Okay. You have to promise not to be mad."

"I don't get mad, I get even," you tell them. They don't know if you're serious or not until you smile. They all giggle, then poke Miss Montana in the back like it's her turn to talk.

"Okay. We dare you to order the cheese tray from room service and eat the *whole* thing!"

That's it? These girls are definitely amateurs. "I knew you guys had a devious streak! Did you know I'm lactose intolerant?" you say, playing along.

They gasp. That threw them for a loop, but it's true. Ever since that one bad night of White Russians and Mudslides at your cousin's wedding you've only been able to digest dairy in small doses.

"You're lactose intolerant?" says Miss Montana, mulling it over. "I guess we can give you an alternative dare . . ."

"That's fair. And if I don't want to do that one I'll just go ahead and do the cheese thing," you say, shrugging. You know it won't come to this—if the cheese plate was all they could come up with, your other choice can't be too scandalous.

"We dare you to skinny-dip in the hotel pool!" Miss Montana exclaims.

"Like, right now?"

"You're darn tootin.'"

"There could be families or guests taking a late night swim!"

"I know they've got one or two swimming pools in Vermont. Don't tell me you haven't taken the plunge oh-nature."

"You mean au naturel," you correct her. She's right—you've skinny-dipped in your day, but never in a hotel pool. Ordinarily, you'd do it in an instant—stripping down and jumping in was practically your major in college. But then your worries were about cold Vermont lakes, not the massive morals contract that you had to sign to compete in Miss Liberty. Not only could you be caught stark naked by pageant officials, they might think you were—gasp—exercising, which is expressly forbidden in the days before the pageant.

Miss Montana's looking less and less friendly. In fact, she's getting annoyed. "No more excuses, Vermont. Pick one."

You'd rather get cheesy than get naked. Turn to page 159.

Nude up and dive in. Take the plunge on page 177.

You decide to keep your enemies close and join the table of Texas the Terrible and her pageant posse.

"I would love to join you," you tell Miss Texas, almost instantly regretting your words. You glance over your shoulder to your shocked girlfriends and mouth the word "sorry." They look at you like you have just agreed to go home with Jeffrey Dahmer.

"Ladies, meet Miss Vermont," Texas introduces you, and gestures like a game-show presenter. "Vermont, meet Miss Liberty's finest. We have Miss New Jersey here, who won her state by a landslide . . ." the beautiful brunette Miss Jersey waves to you with dragonlike fingernails. "And Miss Iowa, the most connected competitor this year." The redheaded Miss Iowa greets you with raised eyebrows and a sneer. "And of course you know last year's Miss Liberty . . ." In an act of supreme graciousness the reigning Miss Liberty puts down her bottle of Pabst Blue Ribbon and stands to shake your hand as she delivers a glittering smile.

"Thanks for letting me sit with you," you say, taking a seat at the end of the table. "I haven't really gotten a chance to meet all of you guys yet . . ."

"Well, the cream rises to the top, if you know what I mean," snaps Miss Iowa. "Tell me, Vermont, how long have you been competing in pageants?"

All eyes are on you. "Actually, the Miss Liberty regionals at the beginning of the year was my first pageant ever." The girls are silent.

"Ev-ah?" asks Jersey, in a horrific accent.

"Yup," you reply. "I entered it on a dare to win a couple cases of beer . . . which I drank wearing my sash and crown."

You newfound friends are starting to look resentful. You can't help but be a little smug about it, though. You are proud that you didn't have to live your life as a series of Miss Junior Misses, Miss Pre-teens, Miss Awkward-phases, Miss Little Misses, and Miss Adorable Toddlers pageants.

"You're practically a virgin," coos Texas. "Honey, you have things to learn!"

"Well, the pageant is tomorrow, and I've made it this far. What could I possibly have to learn?"

"The good news is, you're sitting with us," Jersey says.

"You will never get anywhere hanging out with those filler states," Texas continues, gesturing to your friends. "You'll just have 'loser' written all over you."

"What we are trying to say," says Miss Liberty, sending the table into a hush, "is that the Miss Liberty crown is won *off* the stage, not on the stage. That is what true pageant veterans know." Miss Liberty positively beams kindness and benevolence as she says, "You have managed to make it this far on luck. We want to help you take it to the next level."

"We think you could be one of the final five," Miss Texas starts. "We already know we're going to be. So, if you help us, then we can help you," she says slowly.

"I don't understand," you say, suddenly feeling like you are sitting across the Godfather's desk.

"If you knock someone out for us," Texas explains, "we can knock you in." You wonder if being "knocked in" is kind of like being "jumped in" to a gang—where the gang members beat the hell out of you to welcome you to their posse.

"What do you want?" you ask, cautiously.

Miss Texas pulls out a small pillbox and slides it across the table toward you. "We know for a fact that every girl you came in with is on the rag right now. Something about pheromones and them hanging out together too much." You look over to your state sisters, suddenly grateful you didn't spend all week with them. Delaware and District of Columbia are huddled close, and Nevada is at the bar talking to some guy in a Led Zeppelin T-shirt. "What I want you to do is replace the pills in the bottle of Midol that they share with these pills."

You look down at the pillbox. "What are these?" you ask.

"Come on," huffs Iowa. "You should know what the hell they are. All you do out in your woodsy wonderland state is throw raves and shit."

"You want me to dose them with Ecstasy?" you ask, incredulous.

"Don't make it sound so creepy," says Texas. "They'll end up having the best pageant of their lives. If you take care of these girls, we can handle the rest. I already took care of the Pacific Northwest . . ."

"I got the gals from the Eastern Seaboard," chimes in Jersey.

"And I handled most of the Midwestern states," says Iowa.

You know you are merely a pawn in this treacherous little game. You cannot imagine what mishaps are to befall the girls from other states, and you probably don't want to know. Dosing your friends officially falls under the category of "not cool" in your playbook, but what if you decide not to play along? This is a kill-or-be-killed situation, and perhaps it's better to be on offense rather than defense. Otherwise, you might wake up tomorrow with a torn evening gown, a busted electric guitar, and a system full of illicit drugs.

There is no way you are letting these brats pull you into their twisted game. Don't dose your buds and turn to page 163.

Your gal-pals are about to have the most blissful and ecstatic pageant of their careers. Slip them a few happy pills and turn to page 168.

You can handle a little plate of cheese. It's probably the good stuff, too. You should be over that dairy problem by now, right?

"Who's gonna call room service?" you say with a grin. A little cheer goes up as Miss Montana hops over to the phone.

After half an hour of hearing stories about first kisses and mean teachers, you're ready to stab yourself in the head with the nearest nail file. Mercifully, room service arrives at the door.

"Cheese time!" the girls say, opening the door for a poor, tired room service guy. He's carrying a huge tray—like the size-of-a-large-pizza huge.

"You must have the wrong room," you say, smiling sweetly. "We ordered the cheese plate."

"No you didn't. You ordered the cheese *tray*." He takes the cover off to reveal a massive mountain of various cheese chunks. This is no cute dessert plate of five or six little cheese nibbles, this is the kind of tray that people barely make a dent in at parties.

"This is bullshit you guys, who do you think I am, Miss Wisconsin?" you complain. Montana's already signing the bill. The room service guy makes a quick getaway; now it's just you, a bunch of rabid girls, and a mosaic of cheese cubes.

"Let's go, Vermont!" Miss Montana barks.

You stare at the cheese and then at the girls and know you have no choice. A dare is a dare. You pick up a little toothpick and dig in.

You only make it through half of the cheese tray, apparently there's some medical condition where people can only eat so much dairy before their system shuts down. When you mention the term "projectile vomit," the girls send you back to your room for fear you'll kick it *Exorcist*-style on their bunny slippers. It's two in the morning and you've got a gut full of dairy. You don't even make it to your bed, heading straight for the toilet. And that's where you stay for the next six hours, convulsing and sick, forcing the cheese out of your system. It may be the most disgusting night of your life. You doubt that childbirth is as painful. Not to mention that you can hear your snubbed roommate, Miss Florida, laughing her ass off at your misfortune the whole time.

But, the next morning is a whole different story. You're a little pale and shaky, but after some nondairy food and a fistful of vitamins, you're feeling pretty good. In your dressing room, Miss Nevada, your girlfriend who went out drinking last night, looks like hell. She gives you a once-over.

"What did you do, take water pills?"

"What do you mean?" you ask.

"Check you out girl! You must have lost ten pounds. You look fabulous."

"I wouldn't necessarily call spending all night on the porcelain throne fabulous but on a day like today, I'll take whatever I can get."

You check yourself in the mirror and realize that she's

right. You've re-hydrated like the doctor says to do after a night like yours, but you've definitely lost a little something. If your parents or friends saw you, they'd be horrified and say you look like you've just had mono for a month and forgot to eat.

"Let's go, ladies!" shouts the stage manager. You line up with the other girls and prance onstage like a good little beauty queen. You feel a little lightheaded, like you're floating through the motions. The lights hurt your eyes and the music hurts your ears, but you somehow manage to make it through. When Roddy Topper reads the names of the semifinalists, you're one of them. But it takes you a few moments to process the information. In fact, Miss Nevada has to kick you before you start walking to the winners' side of the stage. You try to look appreciative, but really all you can think about is how great it would be if there was a turkey sandwich waiting for you backstage when this is all over.

You make it through your talent portion, but only barely. Somehow you made Van Halen sound like Yanni. You wonder if anybody really noticed besides the guys running stage crew, who just look at you over their moustaches and shake their heads in shame. You're never quite on track after that, and when Roddy reads the finalists' names, you're not among them. When you get offstage, you rush past a dozen weepy girls and find a bottle of Gatorade. You're gulping down the whole thing when a youngish guy in a sharp suit comes up and extends his hand.

"Hi. I'm Carl Tannenbaum. I work as a network consultant in Hollywood . . ."

"So you're doing God's work," you say dryly.

"We're not that bad," he laughs. "I'm just a guy whose job is to find the next fresh face and drag it back to Los Angeles."

"So why are you talking to me?" you ask, genuinely curious.

"You have a face and a figure that would translate so well on the small screen. My network has a part in an upcoming comedy that would be perfect for you."

"Perfect for *me*?"

"You'd be playing a lawyer at a really crazy law firm who is trying to balance her social life and her professional life and she's charmingly unlucky in love."

"This sounds a little familiar."

"No, it's a totally original idea."

"That's what I meant." He hands you his card and a plane ticket. You thought this might be a hallucination, but this guy is actually for real.

"I'll see you in a week for the screen test," he says with a wink. "And one more thing. This is a little awkward, but it is Hollywood and I'm sure you'll understand. Is it possible for you to drop ten pounds by next week?"

"No problem," you say, your guts churning in rebellion. "I just have to make a quick call to room service."

The End

Drugging girls in bars is strictly for roofie-toting date rapists, not the representative of the great state of Vermont!

What these bitches don't know is that you have watched one too many heist films in your day. You happen to know a thing or two about baiting and switching, playing both sides against each other, and lots of other cool phrases like that. Watch a con artist at work, you think, while reaching for the pillbox.

"I'll do it," you say, shoving the unmarked pillbox into your purse and placing your purse on your lap underneath the table. As you unhook the box, you ask, "So what did you guys do to those hussies from the South?"

"Oh my Gawd," Jersey begins in a hush. "I have a hotel security tape of Miss Georgia and Miss North Carolina going down on each other in the hotel hot tub. You know, all those Southern belle sorority chicks are ga-ga-ga-gay. They're *so* not going to be a problem."

You listen intently as you unscrew a bottle of emergency aspirin in your purse and replace the aspirin pills with the Ecstasy. You put your aspirin in the Ecstasy pillbox—very slick if you do say so yourself. The switch is nearly complete as Miss Iowa finishes telling the tale of how she has loosened the heels of all the Pacific Northwest contestants with a handsaw earlier that night. You hate to admit how well-organized and purely evil these girls are. Terrorist groups would find some dream recruits in them.

You put the pillbox on the table and shake it around, rattling the newly switched pills. You wink at the girls, dramatically push yourself away from the table, and walk over to your friends, the "loser" states. The only girls left are Delaware and District of Columbia—Nevada left through the back door with a handsome trucker and seems unlikely to return anytime soon.

"Hey, Delaware," you shout, so Texas and her evil sisters can hear you, "I have the worst cramps. Do you have a Midol?" You glance over Delaware's shoulder to see a smirking Miss Texas, and several male bar patrons gawking at you like you're a menstrual monster. As she hands you the bottle, you shout, "Oh my God, D.C., over there! Is that Nancy Kerrigan?"

"I *love* her!" Delaware squeals, craning her neck.

"I wanted to be her since I was sixteen!" yells D.C. As the girls scan the crowd for their hero, you make a showy switch of the pills from her Midol bottle with the aspirin for the benefit of Miss Texas, who is clueless about your own switcharoo. You wink at her and slip the bottle back into Delaware's handbag.

Hoping to escape from Miss Texas and her minions, you head to the bathroom, and pass by a table of very cute but grungy looking guys tucked into a booth in the back. As you pass by their table, they hold up cocktail napkins in unison. Each of the napkins has a number scrawled on it. You stop short, realizing they are judging marks. Even though you are disgusted, you must admit that they are pretty high marks: one 8.5, two 10s, and one guy has kindly rated you an 11.

"Very mature, gentlemen," you say, passing by. "That really makes me feel like you respect me as a person."

"But I gave you an eleven!" pleads the one guy. "Come on, Eleven! Sit down and let us buy you a drink." You look over at the guys, who are now sheepishly crumpling up their napkins and looking at you apologetically. One of them pushes out a chair for you.

"Sorry," another guy says. "It was *his* idea."

Somehow, you have managed to get yourself into quite a predicament. You either have to sit at a table of backstabbing beauty-queen harpies or a table of grungies who rate girls on a scale of one to eleven. Like voting in any presidential election, the question is, which is the lesser of two evils?

At least the guys won't rip your evening gown or chop your heels when you're not looking. And they think you're an 11. . . . Sit with the grungies and turn to page 205.

You have had enough scrutiny from male judges to last a lifetime. Tell these guys they are averaging about a 2.5, and join your rivals by turning to page 186.

You're not about to go kiss the room service guy or eat something gross; you'd rather do the whole "truth" thing.

"Truth," you tell them.

"Oooh. Okay. Hmm. Okay. What is the most daring thing you have ever done?"

"Isn't that more of a 'dare' question?"

"She is just so funny!" giggles Miss Montana. Then she turns serious. "You better not lie to us, V-Tee, because if you do, we'll *know.*"

"And you can't say that it was daring to enter Miss Liberty, because we all did that so it doesn't count," points out Miss Louisiana. "We want really daring."

They all turn to you, awaiting your response. You're about to tell them what your most daring moment was, but then you think about it.

There are several things you've done in your life that would qualify as daring. Walking into this pit of vipers was definitely one of them, but you don't think they would appreciate it if you used this occasion as your most daring experience. You're well aware of what your most daring experience is.

It was the fall of your freshman year. You were dating a beautiful art student who liked to paint in oils and sculpt with aluminum, and one day he mentioned that his class was looking for a live model to use in their class. . . .

"Look . . . I don't know . . ." you protest, pushing the memory out of your head.

"Tell us, Vermont!"

You could always lie. You bet these girls have swallowed every lie their boyfriends have told them over the years; why should you be any different?

If you think these girls can't handle the truth, lie your ass off and turn to page 196.

What do you have to hide? These girls will be blown away by how fucking brazen you can be in the name of art. To tell the truth, turn to page 172.

After years of pageants rife with Valium, amphetamines, and diet pills, a little Ecstasy can't hurt these girls. Besides, you don't want to get on the wrong side of Miss Texas. . . .

You grab the little pillbox and leave the table without a word. You are so nervous your fingers are trembling, rattling the pillbox full of drugs. You approach Delaware and D.C. hesitantly, unsure of how you're going to get your hands onto their pills. Delaware whirls around suddenly, startling you.

"Oh, hi!" she gushes. "Hold this!" she chirps, shoving her purse into your chest. "I'm going to learn how to play shuffleboard! I'm so psyched!!!" She skips off to the aging shuffleboard table in the corner of the bar, and D.C. follows her to watch what will certainly be a great moment in sports history.

You sit on a barstool and scope out the bar. Delaware and D.C. are jumping up and down, squealing and throwing sand at the shuffleboard table, oblivious to your imminent deception. Texas, Jersey, Iowa, and Miss Liberty are all watching you with lowered eyes and evil grins. You remove the Midol bottle, empty the contents into your pocket, and refill the bottle with the small pills from the pillbox. Snapping the lid back on the Midol bottle, you slip it into Delaware's purse. You return it to her at the shuffleboard table, and the deed is done. You wish you could feel relief, but you don't. You feel like shit.

"Nice work for an amateur," sneers Iowa.

"Well, tell me what an old-timer like yourself has done," you challenge. "Tell me what you did to the other girls."

All of them lean their heads in toward the center of the table conspiratorially, and begin to spill.

You have not slept a wink since your head hit the pillow, and now the sun is high in the sky and you're due to check in backstage. You drag yourself into the shower, pack up your things, and trudge down to the casino floor. You are now part of a "vast and widespread conspiracy" that undermines everything you have ever believed in. You have never felt so awful and guilty in your entire life.

Backstage, your roommate Miss Florida asks you, "What do you think looks better? The blue contact lenses or the violet ones?" She bats her eyelids to reveal one purple eye and one blue eye. You gaze into her differently colored eyes and tell her that purple is the new blue, but all you can think is this: Miss Florida, sometime during the swimsuit competition your shoulder strap will mysteriously snap, and you will expose yourself to the world.

"Can you help me zip up my leotard?" asks Miss Alaska, on her way to the stage. You zip her up and pray that her eveningwear has maximum coverage, because in several hours she will realize the self-tanner she obsessively applies is laced with red Jell-O powder. She's going to look like a cooked lobster.

You whirl around and watch all the backstage activity. To the casual observer, it looks like your typical pre-show madness: girls running around in various states of undress, clouds of aerosol hairspray, dancers stretching, singers warbling, stagehands hustling about with props in hand. But what you see beneath the surface are evening gowns with tampered zippers, pumps with broken heels, pianos with severed strings, a plate of "good luck" cookies made with chocolate Ex-Lax, and judges who have been blown and bribed.

"I just wanted to wish you good luck!" Miss Delaware appears before you and wraps her arms around you in a warm embrace. "I really think you're going to win," she gushes, "and we're all pulling for you." She reaches into her purse and pulls out the bottle of Midol. "I am *so* on the rag and having cramps from hell. There is no way I am going to be able to pull off my back handspring, double back-tuck, roundoff . . ." she rants, while fiddling with the cap of the tainted bottle.

The only girl you have met this week who honestly wishes you well and is not a full-blown pageant freak is about to accidentally take the illicit drugs that you deliberately gave her. Now is your chance to speak up and make everything right. But what are you going to say? If you tell her now, then she'll think you're the person behind all the acts of sabotage. She could report you to the pageant officials, the judges, and most frighteningly, to all the other girls in the competition. Not only could you be booted out of the pageant, you'd undoubtedly have a mob of angry beauty queens ready to hunt you down and kick your ass.

Bite your tongue and be happy that you are getting through the pageant without serving as the butt of a cruel prank. Avoid the blame and turn to page 180.

You must redeem yourself and undo all the evils that the evil state of Texas has compelled you to do. Repent and turn to page 174.

You don't have anything to hide. You spill your guts to the girls.

"It was my freshman year . . ." You regale them with your story, holding the girls in rapt attention. As you describe your torrid affair, Miss Louisiana begins to blush.

"What do you mean when you say he had the hands of a sculptor?" she asks. You roll your eyes and continue.

". . . so I agree to be a live model for his drawing class."

"I thought you said he worked mainly in oils."

"Which is why he wanted to take drawing! Anyway. So I spend all week at the gym and I show up at his class. There's a sort of old-style lounge chair and a sheet. And they hand me the sheet."

"So you posed naked?" Miss Louisiana whispers.

"Not at first," you say. "I was covered at first, but as the class went on, I felt more and more comfortable. The sheet fell off me at one point and I just never really . . . picked it up."

"You posed naked," Miss Louisiana says, a little louder this time.

"No. I was a nude model for an art class."

"You totally posed *naked*!"

"I totally did not. There are no *Penthouse* issues featuring me, and it's not like the class was all men, either. There were women drawing me as well."

"You're a total lesbian!"

"If I knew this was the way you were going to react—"

"Look, tree hugger, where I come from we keep our clothes on in school," says Miss Montana. The other girls nod in agreement.

"It wasn't a fifth grade class! It was college!" you explain. But these girls are the very definition of "quick-to-judge." As far as they are concerned, you may as well be spread-eagled in *Hustler.*

"I wonder if the pageant officials know about this," muses Miss Louisiana.

And in about thirty minutes you bet your sweet ass they do.

By morning you're flying coach on the way back to Vermont. The news has hit the AP wires, and the whole world is talking about your scandal. One phone call to your ex-boyfriend and you learn that everybody who was in that art class has dug out their old charcoal drawings and put them on eBay. You've given them a way to pay for their next year of school, so that makes you, Miss Vermont, a patron of the arts.

The End

Dreams of pageant gold have turned you into your worst nightmare—they've turned you into Miss Texas. Time for redemption . . .

"Don't do that!" you yell, grabbing the bottle of pills from Delaware's hand. She looks like you've just snatched away her baby.

"What is your problem, V-Tee?" she shrieks. "You do not take Midol from a menstrual woman!"

"This isn't exactly Midol," you say, sheepishly. "It's kind of Ecstasy. Compliments of the Lone Star state. I heard Texas and the other top dogs talking about it last night." Delaware looks skeptical. "They fucked with everything. Look, I'm sorry I didn't tell you earlier."

"Prove it then," she says, still eyeing the Midol like she's going to pry it from your grip.

"Okay," you say, "in about thirty seconds, Wisconsin is going to try to adhesive-spray the butt of her leotard and wind up with an assfull of black spray paint instead." You point over to Miss Wisconsin, dressed in her cheese-themed costume, a swiss-cheese print leotard and a huge foam cheddar wedge on her head. She picks up the can of adhesive and sprays. Sure enough, she coats herself in black paint, and shrieks in horror at the mess.

"How did you know?" Delaware asks.

"Tell you later. We have to hurry if we want to save the

others. We don't have much time." You rush to your makeup kit and hand your emergency tube of Krazy Glue to Delaware. "All the high heels of the Pacific Coast states, and especially the Northwest—go now!" you bark like an army general. "I'll rendezvous with you after I replace the missing springs from Idaho's trampoline."

About thirty minutes later, you have taken the grapefruit out of Missouri's tuba, warned Rhode Island that she is moisturizing her face with Nair, and even found time to run down to the orchestra pit and alert the conductor that Miss Tennessee is to sing an opera aria, and not "Tits and Ass" from *A Chorus Line.* South Dakota's ballet slippers are no longer crawling with fire ants. You have returned Miss Michigan's Seeing Eye dog. All is right in the world once again.

You are so preoccupied backstage averting more than forty near-disasters that your performance onstage is lacking. During the opening number you miss a few steps while breaking the fall of several dancers whose shoes were more wobbly than usual. And you get a major wedgie during the swimwear competition because you were not sure which can of aerosol adhesive was the real deal and which was liquid heat. You don't make it to the top five, but you do manage to seize Arizona's mouthwash bottle before she winds up with a mouthful of Drano.

The next day at the farewell brunch, you gaze up at Miss Iowa, the next Miss Liberty. She waxes poetic to television cameras about making the world a better place by getting pets spayed and neutered. Of course it's repulsive that she won, but at least you feel good about yourself. And all your altruism does not go unrewarded. . . .

"Ladies," Roddy Topper says, tapping a microphone at the front of the room, "will you please give a warm round of applause to the woman you have selected as this year's Miss Congeniality, Miss Vermont!" Just like any good pageant winner, your hands fly to your mouth and your eyes bug out. You forgot about Miss Congeniality! You rush up to the stage to claim your sash and modest bouquet and wave to your dozens of new friends. You mouth the words "thank-you" to them. And you really mean it.

The End

You'd much rather go skinny-dipping than ingest a whole plate full of cheese. At least this way you'll burn calories, not consume them.

"So where's the pool?" you ask.

You tell them this is going to be like a surgical strike—quick, precise, and over in seconds. The stripping down will be done in here to minimize the time you'll have to spend wrestling off your shoes. You take one of those complimentary terrycloth robes, get naked, and run in place to get the adrenaline going. You know how these girls think—you're keeping the robe within arm's reach at all times, and you're making sure you have your own room key with you.

"Are you ready?" Miss Montana says, FunSaver camera in hand.

"Leave the camera. This isn't a Kodak moment."

"Gosh, you're no fun."

"And you're not as dumb as you like to act. So the camera stays. Got it?"

"Got it," says Miss Montana, humbled. The other girls even shoot her looks that make you think she just blew that Miss Congeniality title.

You trot down the hall with the girls until you reach the elevator. Thankfully, it arrives empty. A bunch of rabid beauty queens and a girl in a robe would make a strange sight. The last thing you want is to attract attention.

When you arrive on the swimming pool floor, everything seems quiet. It is pretty late, after all, and if there were kids in the pool, they'd be gone by now. There is a big heavy door at the end of the hall, and the pool is located right behind it. For a moment you think you've been spared—there's no way it will be unlocked.

"It's late, I bet the pool's closed," you say, trying to sound sad.

"Oh mah God it's open!" says Miss Missouri, opening the door. Damn.

You stick your head inside and the only thing you notice is the chlorine smell. No little children, no pageant officials, just silence.

"Okay. You are *all* my witnesses," you say, heading toward the pool.

"Hey, Vermont—" says Miss Montana. "You're the bravest person I've ever met."

You start to say thanks, then remember that Miss Montana's public service platform for Miss Liberty involves kids fighting to survive leukemia.

You untie the robe at the pool's edge. The girls are all crowded at the door, breathless with anticipation. You drop the robe, standing there for a second in your birthday suit. With a quick prayer that the water is not as cold as it looks, you make sure you've got your best form, and dive in.

The water feels pretty great, you have to admit, and swimming naked—well, it's no wonder people like to do it. Plus, it's pageant policy that the girls are not permitted to do any serious exercise the week of the pageant, so this is kind of nice. But by the time you surface, your buzz has been officially killed.

". . . *Run!* They're *coming!*" the girls are shouting. You look up and see them taking off like spooked sheep. On the other side of the poolroom, a couple of men you recognize as two main pageant enforcers are strolling in with their towels. Your options are pretty slim. You can make a run for it, or you can swim across the pool and head for the hot tub. They'll notice you either way, but this is a give-me-Miss-Liberty-or-give-me-death situation.

Run. Run like you've never run before. And do it quick on page 184.

You're going hot-tubbing. Make a dive for it by turning to page 189.

This girl pops Dexatrim like it's Pez. One little hit of Ecstasy can't do much now. . . .

You watch her pop the little white pill in her mouth and chug it down with a healthy slug of Evian.

"You know what?" you tell her. "You should drink a lot of water. I mean a lot. I hear it's great for cramps."

"Really?" Delaware asks.

"Trust me. Hydrate yourself."

You turn and run away before the effects of the Ecstasy kick in. You do *not* want to be around when Miss Delaware starts asking for a hand massage or pawing soft items of clothing. You hurry into your Vermont costume for the opening number—a dairy-themed unitard with a cow tail and a headpiece shaped like cow ears. You scramble up to the stage and into position holding a cardboard cutout of your state in front of you. All fifty girls are on a huge staircase and everyone is arranged to look like a map of the United States.

You look past the girls to Miss Delaware standing several states in front of you. She looks a little goofy with her banking-themed headdress full of dollar bills and silver coins. Then again, you are wearing cow ears. But Delaware is smiling like a kid at Disneyland, and her pupils are starting to dilate. You hope she's going to be okay. "Vermont," she coos, "I love you. You are a beautiful human being."

"Thanks," you mutter, feeling guilty and ashamed. Maybe Dexatrim and Ecstasy aren't so similar after all. . . .

The footlights glow, the orchestra plays its opening chords, and the curtain rises. You are blinded by spotlights and begin to sing the Miss Liberty theme song to an audience of millions. You are smiling brightly and giving what pageant directors call "good expression." Everything starts out beautifully. The staircases move apart and all of the women descend to the stage level to approach the microphone and announce their name and state.

"I'm Amanda Mellinger, from the great state of Kansas."

"My name is Kira Goldberg from Virginia."

"I am Abby Shupe, representing Indiana."

You are descending the staircase to approach the microphone when Delaware catches a heel on a stair. Unsteady from the flashing lights and a system full of drugs, she pitches backward and knocks you on the head with a giant cardboard cutout of the great state of Delaware. You reel forward and try to break your fall, but it is too late. Whap! You land squarely on your face in front of a live audience of millions. You are flat on your stomach, cheek to the stage, when you feel several girls pulling you up to your feet. One of them happens to be your spaced-out friend from Delaware. You brush yourself off and somehow manage to utter your name and state at the microphone, but all you can think about is your humiliating fall—and the fact that Delaware now looks like some kind of saint who helped her spastic and clumsy friend.

They say that once an Olympic ice-skater falls during her routine, she can never mentally recover, and the rest of her performance suffers. This theory certainly holds true for you in the remainder of the pageant. You stumble during the swimsuit competition and can't hit the right chords in your electrical guitar solo during the talent segment. You are not surprised when you don't even make it into the top five.

You are shocked, however, when Delaware is announced as one of the finalists. She sailed through her gymnastics routine like she was on cables, and the judges described her during the swimsuit presentation as "unusually confident and comfortable with her figure." The real kicker comes when Roddy Topper, host of Miss Liberty, asks Delaware her final interview question.

"Miss Delaware," he reads off a cue card, "if you could send one message to the children of the world, what would it be?"

Delaware takes a deep breath and begins, "I would tell all the children of the world to learn to love one another as human beings. That we are all children of the same planet, and that our ability to love one another is what makes humans so special . . ." You inwardly groan as she continues with wild eyes and a cooing voice, "When children learn love, they learn tolerance, and when tolerance exists, hatred ceases to exist. And then the world will be at peace. Love one another is what I would tell the children. Thank you." The audience bursts into impassioned applause, and you think you can see one of the judges wiping a tear from the corner of her eye.

Moments later, Roddy Topper announces, "Meet your new Miss Liberty! Miss Delaware!" Delaware screams with joy but takes ample time to give every other contestant onstage a warm and sincere embrace before she will accept the sash and crown. As she walks down the aisle for her victory march, she mouths the words "I love you, America," to the television audiences. She is ecstatic.

The End

Cowards run. And right now, that's exactly what you are.

You kick down into the water, making like a dolphin. Your robe is on the other side of the pool, if you can only make it in time. Holding your breath, you use all your strength to swim underwater, never breaking the surface. Finally, you touch the opposite wall. When you come up for air, you feel a little faint. Rubbing the chlorine from your eyes, something comes into focus. It's the meanest of the hardcore pageant officials. And he's holding your robe.

"Miss Vermont, I'd recognize that breaststroke anywhere."

"This is not what it looks like . . ." you start to say, then realize there's really no point. "Yes it is. It's exactly what it looks like."

The official press release says that you were caught exercising the night before the competition, a strict no-no. Lucky for you they left out the whole part about you being bucknaked. You return to your state with your head hung low, embarrassed to have been booted from Miss Liberty for such a stupid stunt. When you finally get up the courage to explain it to your mother, she doesn't take it well.

"Honey. If all your friends said they were going to ski off a cliff, would you?"

"Probably," you sigh. "But only if they dared me."

The End

You can stand being judged by judges for a "charitable organization," but by a bunch of hooligans in a bar? You are supposed to be safe here!

"Thanks gentlemen, but I get rated on a scale of one to ten every day. And frankly, I need a break from it."

"Awww, come on," one spiky-haired dude whines. "It's a joke! Lighten up a little. Who do you think you are? Miss Liberty?"

"No," you answer flatly, "I'm Miss Vermont. Fascinating, huh? I could sit here and talk to you all day about the naked pillow fights all of us pageant girls get into every night in our hotel suite, but that would probably bore you. Bye guys." You saunter away and leave the table in shock.

A few moments later you can hear the grunge guys slugging each other and saying, "You are such an idiot dude, why did you chase her away?" and "She's Miss Vermont dude! You don't pull that cocktail napkin shit on her!"

You unenthusiastically rejoin your table of the elitist pageant brats. "Who were those skate rats?" Texas sneers, "I can't believe you even *breathed* near them."

"My Gawd," Jersey wails. "It looks like they crawled out of a sew-wah!"

"Are we ready to meet some *real* gentlemen?" the usually mute Miss Liberty asks. All the girls nod in unison and gather their things.

"Please get me out of this white-trash hellhole," Iowa mutters. She turns to you and says, "You coming or what?"

You grab your purse and follow them to the exit of the bar. In the parking lot you are greeted by a long black stretch limousine, which looks conspicuous among the dusty pickup trucks. A chauffeur hops out of the front seat, walks around the limo, and opens the passenger door. Half a dozen tuxedo-clad tall-dark-and-handsomes step out of the car.

"Ladies?" one of them motions to the limo. You look over to the girls in confusion. Where did these guys come from? How did they know to find you here? They must be friends of Miss Liberty or something, but it just seems too bizarre. You look over the men again. There is no denying they are drop-dead lovely; each one with perfect olive skin, deep dark eyes, and pitch-black slicked-back hair. They look so similar, they could be brothers.

"Who are they?" you whisper to Miss Texas.

"Pageant patrons, honey. They hold the Miss Liberty purse strings," she says through clenched teeth, "so stop asking stupid questions and get in the damn car." You watch Miss Liberty kiss one of the gentlemen on the cheek and climb in the car. Iowa follows.

The rest of the women approach the limo, but your feet are still stuck to the ground. There's something suspicious about this whole arrangement; it just seems too good to be true. Maybe, you think, this is some elaborate scheme, and you are the butt of some practical joke.

On the other hand, you are with four other women, so it must be safe, right? And if these men are who Texas claims they are, you may actually find yourself in a very lucrative position. You may be able to manipulate or seduce your way into wearing that Miss Liberty sash and crown. Plus, you have never turned down a limo ride before, and holy shit—they could have a minibar!

One more minute with these pageant bitches is not worth all the tall-dark-and-handsomes in the state of Nevada. Let the limo roll without you and turn to page 199.

Miss Liberty is just like prom! Dancing, sequined gowns, and now a limo ride! Climb in for a ride by turning to page 193.

It's hot, it's bubbly, and it's any port in a storm.

You leap out of the pool with such skill and stealth that you wonder if you should maybe consider the Navy Seals. Just as the pageant enforcer guys are concentrating on taking off their watches, you do a dive roll and—splash! You're in the hot tub.

"Nice entry," a male voice says through the steam. Oh God. You're not alone.

The steam clears and you can see a good-looking older man lounging across the hot tub. He's one of those tanned, cute, and distinguished older men who seem to handle themselves well in any situation. Hell, a naked beauty queen just did a dive roll into the hot tub in front of him and he takes it in stride.

"I'm not supposed to be here," you explain.

"I gather that. Which means you must be one of the girls in the Miss Liberty Pageant." He glances at the enforcers, who walk past the hot tub and barely give you a glance. Both of them jump in the pool and start doing laps. You're home free.

"Can I tell you a secret?" you say, slightly high on adrenaline.

"I've kept many women's secrets."

Okay, whatever that means. You tell him anyway. "I'm Miss Vermont."

"What's your talent?"

"I play Van Halen's 'Hot for Teacher' on electric guitar."

"Platform?"

"Teaching agriculture and donating livestock to impoverished families in Africa so they can survive."

"Thank God, I thought you were going to say 'abstinence' or something," he chuckles.

"Already taken. But my real first choice was medical marijuana. It's just too controversial."

"With a name like Miss Liberty, you'd think it would be all about medical marijuana," he says, still laughing.

"I know! To tell you the truth, I thought it was the 'Miss Libertarian' pageant and I entered by accident," you joke. Pretty soon both of you are cracking up.

You end up spending the rest of the night in the Jacuzzi with this guy, waiting for the pageant assholes to finish training for the Ironman. It takes forever, but the time flies. There's something cool about this guy. He's older, sure, but you're sitting there naked and he hasn't once ogled you or even glanced at your breasts. If he hadn't told you such hilarious stories about his ex-wives, you'd think he was gay.

"You know," he says after an hour, "there are more exciting topics in the world, but you haven't asked me what I do for a living."

"So," you say, playing along, "what do you do for a living?"

"I'm Harlan Randall. I work for Mr. Hefner."

"*The* Mr. Hefner?"

"The one and only. Every year he sends a scout to the Miss

Liberty Pageant and every year we come back empty-handed. Either the girls aren't right or they're too conservative or they just don't have the attitude we want, but Hef has always believed this was a great place to scout."

"Miss Texas would do it in a second."

"Miss Texas is probably going to win tomorrow. The problem with scouting Miss Liberty is once the girls win, they won't ever come to us. They'd be written off by the pageant nazis. But you, here, landing in my Jacuzzi and actually knowing the difference between a Libertarian and a librarian . . . you're our girl."

"You want me to pose?"

"I want to offer you a million dollars to pose. That girl from *Survivor* got half that. But I see a real future in you."

Maybe it's the hot water and the dehydration or maybe it's the relief from being free of Miss Montana and her posse, but you hear yourself saying something you never thought you would: "Where do I sign?"

A year later you're standing on Hef's lawn, being crowned Playmate of the Year. It's been a surreal year to say the least, and for the first half of it your parents barely spoke to you. But now that you've got a gig hosting MTV's hottest new game show and a role in Steven Segal's comeback film, they've come around. You had to drop out of the pageant, so you'll never know if you would have ended up as Miss Liberty or not. Sometimes you stay up at night in your kick-ass Hollywood Hills bungalow, staring out at the city lights, and you wonder . . . and then you look at your brand-new Maserati and the wondering stops.

The End

The thought of an in-limo minibar is even more seductive than the handsome gentlemen. You cannot pass up this ride. . . .

You climb into the back of the stretch limo and slide down onto a long leather bench. You smile, noticing a fully stocked minibar, complete with iced champagne and expensive liquors in crystal carafes.

"Drink?" one of the stunning gentlemen offers.

"Champagne, please." He pops open a bottle of Dom and pours you a glass. Across the limo cab, Texas, Jersey, and Iowa have all cuddled up next to their suitors. The gentleman with the champagne slides into the seat next to you.

"I have heard wonderful things about you, Miss Vermont. It is a pleasure to finally make your acquaintance," he says, handing you the glass. "My name is Taj." You coyly introduce yourself and offer your hand, which he gently kisses.

"So why do we get the royal treatment?" you ask, between slugs of bubbly.

"We are, how do you say? Benefactors of the Miss Liberty Pageant. Every year we track down the most beautiful and stunning women in the competition. These women become international representatives for us." You nod like you understand what he is saying, but you are seriously confused. He tops off your champagne as he continues, "We would like you to join our little circle. You would have years of all-expenses-paid trips around the globe, representing our jewelry companies, fragrance companies, apparel companies . . ."

"So, it's like being a spokesmodel?" you ask.

"In a way," Taj says, "it is more like being in public relations." He pulls out a huge contract and places it on your lap. You look at him in confusion.

"I can play guitar, solve a Rubik's Cube, and shotgun a beer, but I can't for the life of me read a contract," you tell him.

"You can have your lawyer look at it when you return home," he says. He tops off your umpteenth glass of bubbly and adds, "but if you sign it now," he gets close and whispers in your ear, "I guarantee you will win tomorrow. We've looked at the other girls, and we are in agreement that we would prefer to offer you the crown first."

Maybe it's the champagne, the limo, the handsome foreign dudes in tuxes, or maybe you are just plain-old greedy for the crown. You sign.

"Meet your new Miss Liberty, Miss Vermont!" Roddy Topper yells. You grab your cheeks in mock surprise and twitter, "Thank you, thank you." The tiara is placed on your head, the sash is fastened around your gown, and you are given a ridiculously large bouquet of roses to carry down the catwalk as Roddy sings, "Here she is, Your Miss Li-ber-ty. She's every girl's childhood fan-ta-sy . . ."

The next morning you find a gift waiting for you outside your hotel door. It is a large package with the unmistakable

Chanel logo on the lid. You open the package to find a stunning pantsuit and a bundle of airline tickets. From the looks of it, next year you will be flying to the Middle East, and taking a private plane to a place called Brunei. The contract you signed last night is also in the bundle, with a passage highlighted in yellow marker:

"You are to begin service to his royal highness, the Sultan of Brunei, as one of his palace attendants, for six months immediately following your reign as Miss Liberty. First-class airfare, accommodations, and meals shall be provided by the Sultan . . ."

The contract goes on and on. You grab the Chanel suit and stroke the silky fabric, absorbing the situation. Taking a deep breath, you recall some article you read in *Cosmo* years ago, about American women who go to the Middle East to live in a harem with dozens of other women in the palaces of royal sultans. Their entire lives consist of working out all day, putting on evening gowns each night, and attending the same party in the same ballroom night after night after night. Ironically, it kind of sounds like reliving the Miss Liberty Pageant every single day.

The End

There is no way in hell you're going to tell these girls something you've barely told your real friends. Sometimes you need to lie.

"Okay. There was this one time that these friends of mine and I were out driving in my neighborhood, and it was one of the hottest days of the year. And this is Vermont. So we decided to sneak into our neighbor's yard and jump in their pool. Anyway . . ." you pause for effect, "we almost did. But instead we went to Baskin-Robbins!" The girls look unenthused. Miss Montana especially.

"I thought you were the wild and crazy one," complains Miss Louisiana. "That's why we invited you!"

"Well, that's just my . . . image," you try.

"Ugh. Whatever. Look—let's forget Truth or Dare and just get ready for tomorrow. All this stuff is stressing me out," Montana grouses.

You're in for an eye-opening night. Miss Montana proceeds to go to her closet and brings out a massive plastic case. It's huge, probably built to carry nukes or something. Miss Montana calls it her "toolbox." Inside are beauty products that would frighten anybody with half a brain. She has bizarre zit remedies, hair removers, skin shiners, cellulite-melting devices, hand waxers, hair volumizers, just about anything you've seen on television and everything they would never show you on television for fear of being sued by the Better Business Bureau.

"Are you girls sure you really need all this stuff?" you ask. The room quiets as if you just suggested that they assassinate the president.

"Look, V-Tee, you know what this pageant's about? It's about any edge you can get. You know how bike racers shave their legs and how swimmers wear certain swimsuits?" asks Miss Montana.

"Or how sometimes you need somebody else to take your SATs for you?" adds Miss Louisiana.

"You can lose by a fraction of a point," Montana says. "Do you want to take that chance? I don't."

By the end of the night you've learned more about beauty and how to increase your bust size than any woman should ever know. The only person who would know more than Miss Montana would be a drag queen, and it would be a close call. You leave the room at a late hour, with your head spinning. You really don't see any way you can beat these girls; they've got plans, techniques, and experience beyond your imagination.

The next morning, you're a wreck. Your roommate Miss Florida is a chipper little psychotic mess and when you tell her how freaked-out Miss Montana made you, she just looks at you funny.

"I mean, do you think I should tape my boobs together?" you ask her.

"Yes! And Vaseline your teeth! I mean, that Montana girl's right. It's all about fractions of points. If my mother taught me anything, she taught me that," Miss Florida says, then starts sneezing uncontrollably while plucking her nose hairs. You are totally screwed.

You make a deal with yourself. You'll try *one* of these beauty tricks. If it works, then you're golden, but if it doesn't, you'll at least feel like you improved your chances of winning.

So you've never taped your boobs together, now's your big chance! You could be a winner by cleavage on page 218.

The Vaseline on the teeth—there's an old trick that even your mom has heard of. And if somebody died from it, you'd have heard about it, so slather it on and smile on page 203.

A limo full of vaguely foreign men screams "call girl" to you. You bid the gents adieu and head back into the bar.

"Oh my God," gushes Delaware, "you will not believe how much I *rule* at shuffleboard!" She hands you a green-tinted cocktail and continues, "If I had known about this sport earlier, I would totally have made it my talent. I mean, rhythmic gymnastics is so 1980s. Shuffleboard is the future!" She leads you to a table, and you see that some sort of elaborate drinking game has been set up.

"Sit down V-Tee!" D.C. shouts. "We are playing a drinking game called 'Categories.' It's so fun! All you have to do is go around in a circle and name a thing in a category." She pours you a drink and continues, "Like if I say '*Simpsons* characters,' then you have to say Bart, or Marge, or Apu. Get it? Whoever fucks up drinks."

You sit down at the table with a smug grin. If there is one thing a girl learns while coming of age in Vermont, it's how to hold her drinks. These girls are toast.

"Okay," says Miss Delaware, "let's begin. First category is: names of former Miss Liberties!"

They start pounding on the table in unison and rattling off names of former winners. You are ashamed that you can't recall a single name of a Miss Liberty ever, except that chick who wound up in *Penthouse* and caused a national scandal. Every time it's your turn, you are forced to take a slug of your toxic cocktail. The game continues around and around the table until these girls are naming Miss Liberties from the era when chicks wore bloomers. You end up slugging down two cocktails within five minutes.

"Okay," Delaware says, "next category is: beauty pageants for girls ages twelve and under!" You audibly groan.

"Miss Sugarplum!" screams D.C.

"Bouncing Baby Beauty!" yells Delaware.

"Junior Miss?" you try.

"Drink V-Tee!!! Drink!" they yell. You slug back more of the mysterious alcoholic concoction.

The girls continue to rattle off names like "Miss Gingerbread," "American Pre-Preteen," and "Terrific Toddlers," and you are forced to keep drinking until the room goes sideways. The last thing you remember is Miss Delaware yelling, "Next category is: facial scrubs!"

"Vermont? Vermont? Are you alive?" You pry your eyelids open and make out the fuzzy image of your roommate, Miss Florida, hovering above your face.

"Waaa-eerr . . ." is all you can manage to mumble. Your head is pounding and you take stock of your situation. You are definitely back in your hotel room, thank God, but you have no clue as to how you got here. You are in the clothes you wore the night before, on your bed, on top of the comforter. Your purse is still slung around your shoulders and your mouth feels like it's full of warm, dry fur.

Your roommate hands you a tall glass of Reno's finest tap water and two pills. "Here," she says, "take these, and drink this. We have to be at the theater in half an hour." She sniffs the air and scolds, "You reek of booze. You better get in the shower."

You lift yourself out of bed, stumble to the bathroom, and run the tub. You catch a glimpse of yourself in the mirror and recoil in horror. Your eyes are bloodshot to hell, your hair is matted in a bizarre triangular shape, and your face is covered with dried drool. You hop into the steaming hot shower and try to wake up. In the shower, you give yourself your morning-after pep talk, and try to snap yourself to attention.

The water cascades down your body and your muscles loosen. The streams of hot water run through your hair and tickle your face. You pull out the soap and start to lather up. The soap feels good. Really good. Your limbs begin to tingle and you start moving and swaying around to an imaginary beat. Suddenly, you feel like the most gorgeous, sexy, and confident woman ever. You are filled with a great sense of happiness and joy for no apparent reason.

You towel off and look in the mirror. Your pupils are dilated beyond belief, and you are grinning goofily. You weren't even aware of it. You brush your teeth, and the sensation is incredibly refreshing and exciting. Something strange is going on here. "Um, what were those pills you gave me?" you inquire to Miss Florida, as you are getting dressed in your incredibly soft clothes.

"I just took the aspirin out of your purse and gave you

that," she replies. You glance down at the aspirin bottle and the night comes streaming back to you. The pills! The aspirin and the Ecstasy!

"Oh God," you shriek. "Oh God, no!"

You look at Florida in horror. "Are you all right?" she asks.

"Yes," you gulp. "I'm ecstatic."

The pageant turns out to be one of the most surreal and beautiful days of your life. You aren't sure if you got all the dance steps right in the opening number, but you don't care. Parading around in your Vermont unitard holding a cardboard cutout of your state gives you such a rush of state pride, you almost burst out in tears. And as your Van Halen electric guitar solo powerfully rips through the theater, you swear you can actually *see* the sound of the notes that you strum. When your name is not called to join the final five, you look at the women who will go on to win the pageant, and you feel like a proud mother. You love those girls. And one of them is going to win. And for the first time in this whole pageant experience, you realize it is not about winning or losing. It's really all about all these incredible, incredible, women whom you have had the privilege of meeting. And that's not just the drugs talking, man.

The End

202

Vaseline seems like a safe choice. Petroleum never killed any—okay, bad example.

You've made it through most of the pageant without incident. In fact, if you weren't feeling so doom-and-gloom, you'd think you'd done pretty well so far. When Roddy Topper reads your name among the semifinalists you're thrilled, but your head's not really in the game. You keep looking over at Miss Montana and her posse and you wonder if they have it all wrapped up. You're the new kid on the block; these girls know the neighborhood like the back of their Borghese-gloved hands.

You're standing in the wings with a jar of Vaseline, waiting for your cue to go onstage so Roddy Topper can ask you his canned question. You uncap the jar, recoiling from the chemical grossness. It's all about winning, right? You stick your manicured index finger into the gook and bring out a hefty dollop. You smear the stuff across your teeth and smile into the nearby mirror. It kind of works. The taste of the Vaseline is so foul you couldn't stop smiling if you tried. And it gives your teeth a chemical glint.

"How do I look?" you ask a cute young stagehand.

"Like a winner," he says with a wink. What a sweetie.

". . . Miss Vermont!" you hear from the stage.

"That's my cue," you say, heading into the light.

Onstage, everybody is applauding as you do your adorable

wave and your half-confident, half-catwalk stride to the micro-phone. When you get there, you take a deep breath. And something's wrong. You don't show it—you *can't* show it—but you can't breathe. You've inhaled the glob of Vaseline and it's sitting in your windpipe. You want to cough but you can't, not now—

"Tell us," Roddy is saying, his face swimming in front of you, "how would you solve the crisis in the Middle East?"

Oh God. Not only can you not breathe, but that has got to be one of the most difficult questions facing mankind, and there is no way in hell you're going to be able to give a good answer with a glob of petroleum jelly in your throat. Your mind pauses on the irony of your situation—issues with petroleum, the Middle East, how such a small piece of land can cause such big problems. . . . What are you going to do?

You'd rather upchuck backstage than become immortalized on the internet as the "barfing beauty queen." Run into the wings on page 208.

It may be possible to hack up and spit out a glob of jelly in a ladylike fashion. Didn't they teach you that in finishing school? Cough it up on page 213.

Rejoining Miss Texas and her posse would be like jumping into a lake full of piranhas. You'd rather take your chances with these grungy kids. . . .

"Are you really here for Miss Liberty?" asks Mr. Eleven, pouring you a beer. You take a seat, and wonder if that's the best line this guy can come up with.

"Yes," you say, slightly annoyed, "I really am. Are *you* here for Miss Liberty?"

"Actually," one of the guys begins, "we kind of are. We're the band, Firewire. We play our new single during the 'Tribute to Liberty' montage while the girls put on their evening gowns."

"We're just breaking out, and we have a new CD, so our record company thought it would be really good exposure," adds a guy in a tone that says "don't think we're sellouts for playing a beauty pageant." You look at the guys and recognize them from a video you saw recently on MTV. It was one of those typical sullen videos shot in an abandoned warehouse, and the song was some overly sensitive yet intense meditation on divorce.

"So you're the new edgy yet heartthrobby band of the month," you tease.

"Yeah," says Mr. Eleven, "we suck. We're total whores. But what else are a couple of philosophy majors going to do with their lives?" He grins and you are suddenly disarmed. Grungy or not, this kid is pretty cute. He stretches out his hand to you and says, "I'm Tommy. Lead vocals."

"Miss Vermont," you say, "Eleven." There is an awkward moment of silence as the two of you goofily grin at each other. Why are you so nervous? You take a sip of your beer and try to relax.

One hour and two pitchers of beer later, one of the band members whaps Tommy on the back and says, "Time to go, dude."

"Listen, Vermont," Tommy says, leaning a little too close, "I have my own car here and we're staying at the same hotel. Why don't you let me give you a ride back?" You look at him skeptically. "I will be on my best behavior," he adds, "I promise."

"I really don't know," you start. "I mean I came with a bunch of other girls . . ." You look around the bar and realize that the only remaining patrons are an old man shooting pool by himself, and a drunk guy sleeping on the bar. God, it's later than you thought.

"We have the bus out back too," says another band member. "You could come ride with us instead, if you want." He jokes, "In the car, Tommy might try to get freaky on you."

You smile and look back over to Tommy. He seems trustworthy and non-threatening, like all the stars on the cover of *Tiger Beat* magazine. I mean, would you be afraid to accept a ride home from Ricky Schroeder? On the other hand, you may feel safer in a bus full of people, and you have never been on a real tour bus before. . . .

If you don't accept rides from cute guys you don't know, then you will have no one to blame but yourself when you die alone. Get in the car with Tommy and turn to page 215.

You always wanted to play rock 'n' roll groupie. Here is your chance—and without all the degrading sex and dangerous drugs! Get on the bus and turn to page 210.

You would rather choke and pass out backstage instead of on national television.

Roddy waits for your answer, smiling like a jackass. You hold up your finger like "give me a minute," then turn on your heel and run offstage. The audience gasps in horror.

You're so near collapsing offstage that you run head-on into a really cute and totally *naked* young guy. One look at his well-endowed body and the shock propels the Vaseline glob-ule from your throat. You faint.

Seconds later you come to, and are able to focus on the face of the young naked guy, who happens to be the same cute young crew guy who winked at you earlier. He smiles at you, a little relieved.

"I thought I was going to have to do mouth-to-mouth," he says.

"That wouldn't have been so bad . . ." you murmur, won-dering if that floaty feeling is due to the lack of oxygen in your brain or the lack of imperfection in this guy. "Can I ask you something personal?" The crew guy nods. "Why are you naked?"

"I was gonna streak the pageant," he says with a smirk. "I've been planning it for months."

"Why?"

"This might sound stupid, but it's a bet. I'm doing all this for a case of beer."

"Me too!" you laugh. "Ohhh. And I ruined it!" you moan, thinking about how cool it would have been to be the contestant onstage when a guy streaked. Everybody knows that David Niven was onstage when the Oscars were streaked in the 1970s and you totally would have made it onto the Trivial Pursuit cards.

"Nah, don't worry about it," he says, helping you to your feet. "I'm a sucker for women in distress."

He quickly puts his pants on as the stage manager rushes up, thinking you've died a horrible death. Pretty soon pageant officials surround you, examining you, asking you what year it is. You tell them you want to keep going, but you're too weak to continue after they come back from the commercial break. Besides, now your makeup is a mess and you've got more carnal things on your mind. . . .

"Do you need somebody to sit with you for the rest of the show?" asks one of the pageant officials.

"I've got somebody," you say, winking at the cute crew guy. He extends a hand and you take it. "If you'll just tell me your name . . ."

"Richard," he says, grinning. "But my friends call me Dick."

You smile wide. But this time it's without the help of Vaseline.

The End

You always wanted to see the inside of a real tour bus—and now you will, you little band slut.

You skip toward the Firewire tour bus as Tommy drives off onto the highway. This is the first time you have been on a tour bus—not for lack of trying, mind you. You recall an incident several lifetimes ago when you promised a roadie sexual favors to get backstage at Aerosmith. But you don't really count that since you were under the age of eighteen and had been drinking Slurpees spiked with vodka all night. You pull back the front door of the bus expecting a modern spread of leather seating, electronic equipment, and a gourmet kitchen. No such luck.

The tour bus looks like the moving dorm room from hell. The couches look like they were found in a garage sale; the television has a wire hanger for an antenna and a tangle of Xbox cords strangling it; the minifridge looks too frightening to open; and every surface is covered with fast-food wrappers, ashtrays, and ashtrays fashioned from fast-food wrappers. The bus starts to roll out and you are not sure where to sit. This is not the glam cocktail-swilling environment you were anticipating. Now you know why Tommy drives his own car, and you have newfound respect for him.

You walk to the back of the bus and see a beautiful Fender guitar propped up on a stand. "May I?" you ask one of the band members. He shrugs and nods. You pick up the guitar and pluck a few strings. You will be playing Van Halen's "Hot for Teacher" in front of millions of viewers tomorrow afternoon for the talent portion of the pageant, and you need all the practice you can get. You fish around in your purse for your lucky pink pick, and rip into the opening chords. This is one of the finest instruments you have ever had the pleasure of playing, and you let yourself really dig in to the solo. You are exhilarated and confident with your act when you finish the song.

You look up to see three extremely shocked band members. They are staring at you like they have just watched you turn water into whiskey. "That is the hottest thing I have ever seen in my entire life," says one of the guys.

"Um, I think I'm in love," says another. The grungy trio kind of mutters to one another under their breaths and nod their heads.

In unison they ask, "Wanna join our band?"

Six months later you are the lead guitarist and sometimes vocalist of the hot new rock band, Firewire. Turns out that these guys were not a fluke after all—they are not only worshipped by teens, but heralded by critics. You are quite a sensation yourself, and the media is constantly speculating on your relationship with Tommy, the bandmate you share your mike—and your bed—with. As a cover story in *Rolling*

Stone will soon reveal, you went to the Miss Liberty Pageant seeking prize money, but didn't even make it to the final round. But you did find fame, fortune, love, and rock 'n' roll along the way.

The End

"The show must go on" is what they always say, and why shouldn't you follow that advice?

You put on that hmmm-let-me-think-about-that face you've practiced so well. You hope Roddy hasn't noticed that your eyes are watering and you haven't actually breathed in about thirty seconds. You silently try to push the glob of Vaseline up through your trachea, but you emit a tiny little baby burp. When amplified over the microphone and the theater's sound system, the burp sounds like a roar.

Roddy is looking at you with concern, and you place your hand over your mouth as you begin to hack and cough. You double over, trying to catch your breath. You haven't coughed this hard since that time you tried out your roommate's four-foot gravity bong—and that time you were rewarded with a six-hour high. Your vision goes blurry; you drop to your knees, suffocating. You must also be hallucinating, because before you pass out into darkness, you swear you see a naked man running across the stage. . . .

Your Miss Liberty Pageant will live in infamy forever. Not because you passed out, or because you were the first contestant to play a Van Halen song for your talent. No, your Miss Liberty Pageant will live in infamy because it was the only nationally televised beauty pageant to be streaked. That's right, you weren't crazy after all. That was a naked man racing across the stage. Personally, you're proud that even though you were suffocating to death, you took the time to momentarily admire his package.

Pageant officials assumed that you were so horrified by the sight of a naked man that you fainted. Although you never got your chance to air your views on how to solve the crisis in the Middle East, you were rewarded second runner-up, which was totally out of pity.

Your friends have not been so forgiving. They too assume that you passed out from the shock of seeing a nuded-up dude, and they will never let you live it down. In fact, it has become somewhat of a clichéd prank for your guy friends to randomly streak your living room while you're watching TV, or any restaurant you may happen to be having dinner in. Which is fine with you. At least you know where all your male friends rank in the talent competition.

The End

They always talk about devastating tour bus crashes on **Behind the Music.** *In the interest of your personal safety— and personal curiosity—you take the ride with Tommy.*

You hop into Tommy's convertible Viper, and pull out onto the dark highway back toward downtown Reno. He fumbles around with the CD player, and you take a moment to really examine his face. His profile is nearly perfect, his curly brown hair flops in the wind, and he has unusually long eyelashes for a guy. No wonder he landed on the cover of *Spin.* Depressing lyrics and angry riffs may appeal to the young guys of America, but his looks certainly appeal to women. Music fills the car—and you are shocked. It's not some asshole rock band, it's Marvin Gaye.

"What? No lame asshole rock?" you ask. "No Korn? No Papa Roach? No Firewire?"

He runs a hand through his floppy hair and laughs. "God, I hate that bullshit. We never started out thinking we would play anthems of preteen angst. I guess that's how it works though."

You nod sympathetically. "I never in a million years thought I would be competing in a beauty pageant. I've been a feminist since I was in diapers!"

"I was in the jazz ensemble!" he says.

"Six months ago, I thought exfoliation was a criminal offense!" you add.

"I thought TRL was a disease!" he yells. You are both laughing like idiots by the time he pulls up to the hotel. "If you don't mind, I'll drop you off here. I don't want to get recognized walking in the front, so I sneak in the back way."

"Thanks for the ride. Maybe I'll see you tomorrow?" you ask hopefully.

"We're supposed to 'stay away' from the pageant girls. But I won't stay away from you." He leans over and plants a sweet kiss on your cheek. You climb out of the car and walk away. It takes all your strength not to look back at him.

The following afternoon, you are sitting backstage in the massive dressing room that the contestants use for primping and preening. The air is thick with a mixture of aerosol hairspray and nerves. You are in the delicate process of layering lipstick and translucent powder when you see a man's reflection in the mirror behind you. He is wearing sunglasses and a baseball cap and he has a single flower in his hand that looks like one of the ones from the massive vase at the casino entrance. You recognize his curly brown hair peeking out of his cap, and turn around to greet him.

"Tommy!" a voice shrieks. "Tommy, oh my God you guys! Look!" A frantic Miss Georgia runs up to him, and practically paws his chest. "You guys, come here!" She waves her hands and some of the other Southern girls surround him.

"Firewire is *so* my new favorite band," purrs Miss South Carolina.

"Your song 'Home of Pain' really changed my life," coos Miss Alabama.

"And I just loved your new video. We can't wait to hear you sing tonight," says North Carolina, batting her eyelashes. Tommy looks over their shoulders and gives you a pleading look that says, "Help!" You would love to walk over there and give Tommy a huge hug just to see the shocked faces of all the Southern girls.

Suddenly, Fanny Mae, the pageant queen bee and head of the morality squad, confronts you. "Vermont," she chirps, "I wanted to talk to you about your talent selection of 'Hot for Teacher,' and its implications vis-à-vis the American educational system . . ." She is droning on, and you are not sure how to excuse yourself and go rescue Tommy without being obvious. And do you really want to be caught canoodling with this rock star under her nose? And how would you explain to her how the two of you know each other? She may find out that you snuck out last night, and that could spell a quick suspension from the pageant.

Blow off Fanny Mae and go rescue your rocker by turning to page 221.

If Tommy's going to be a rock star, he'd better get used to fighting off mobs of rabid women. Let him fend for himself by turning to page 223.

If it worked for Julia Roberts in* Erin Brockovich *it can work for you! Tape those boobs up!

You are backstage before the pageant, padding around with curlers in your hair, wearing slippers and a robe that says "Vermont" across the back, like some boxer. A vision of beauty you are not. But all that is about to change. You scour the backstage area for an ACE bandage, or anything that you can use to boost your cleavage. You are in the area where the stagehands raise the curtains when you spot a big silver roll of duct tape! This will be perfect! You slip the tape in your robe pocket and scamper to the ladies' room.

You stand in a bathroom stall, robe around your waist, boobs in one hand, tape in the other. This is really frigging hard to do alone. How are you supposed to peel tape, lift boobs, and apply tape upside down? Several minutes of tugging and pushing and pulling, you have finally evened out your cleavage and lifted it to new heights. And let me tell you, these girls were not kidding. This shit works. You could rest a cup and saucer on these bad boys. . . .

Hours later, you are at the head of the pack! Your talent performance was spectacular, your evening gown was stunning, and your answer to your interview question about the Israeli-Palestinian crisis was pure gold, baby. But what really put you over the top was the swimsuit competition. No one even came close to you, and you have a feeling you owe it all to your gravity-defying breasts.

Onstage, you clutch the hand of Miss California, the only other remaining contestant. At the microphone, Roddy Topper opens the envelope with the winner's name. "Ladies and gentlemen," he booms, "your new Miss Liberty, Miss Vermont!" A wave of relief washes over you. You did it! Your head is crowned, you are handed a massive bouquet of roses, and you walk down the catwalk toward the audience. Even though you swore to yourself that you wouldn't cry, you get a lump in your throat and start to mist up.

Later, in your hotel room, which is now an upgraded presidential suite, you toss down the flowers, scepter, sash, and crown and start peeling off your clothes. You feel several pounds lighter after removing the beaded gown, and several pounds fatter once you peel off the super-binding control-top panty hose that have kept you sucked in for hours. You go to the bathroom and examine your silver plated chest. You figure this is just like ripping off a Band-Aid. Better to do it in one swift motion, no? You silently count to three, grab one end of the tape, and *rip*!

"Yooooowwwwweeemuutherrrrfuuuckershitshitshit-shit!!!!" you scream at the top of your lungs. You have managed to remove the tape, but you have removed some of your breasts too. Your chest is red and raw and looks like it's missing several layers of very sensitive skin. The throbbing pain and burning sensation is not unlike getting bikini waxed over and over and over again. You pop four Advil, cover yourself in cocoa butter, and hope for the best.

It's a good thing that you won five thousand dollars of discretionary spending money at the Miss Liberty Pageant. You will need it to pay all the microderm specialists it takes to grow back several layers of breast skin over the course of the next year.

And who said being a beauty queen wasn't glamorous?

The End

The sheer terror of being surrounded by so much big hair may be detrimental to your new friend . . . go give your rock star pal a hand.

"Excuse me Fanny Mae," you say as sweetly as possible, "I was just going somewhere."

"Young lady," she clucks, "don't you know it is rude to interrupt a lady, much less a superior? Certainly you read the Miss Liberty etiquette handbook. And as for this obscene song you wish to play, I must urge you to reconsider . . ."

You brush her aside and walk past her toward Tommy. He is now being forced to pose for a photo with Miss Tennessee, who is jumping up and down and weeping tears of joy. You push your way through the sea of sequined evening gowns and helmeted hairdos. Tommy spots you and a flood of relief washes over his face, which has been covered with hot-pink lipstick marks. "Hi Vermont," he says, handing you the now crushed flower, "I just wanted to wish you luck and let you know how great last night was."

Accepting the mangled flower, you flirt, "You better get out of here before my chaperone catches you . . ."

"Excuse me!" A shrill Southern accent shrieks behind you. "What is going on?"

"Oh my God," a scandalized Miss South Carolina whispers, "that little slut is screwing the band."

"Ugh! What a little whore!" screams North Carolina. "You are such a star fucker!"

221

Miss Alabama pulls Fanny Mae over by the arm and points at you and Tommy. "Is there not a strict rule about fraternization during pageant week?" she whines to Fanny Mae. "It's just not fair!"

Fanny Mae looks at you, Tommy, and your crushed flower in disgust. "Vermont," she scolds, "first you want to drag obscene music into this revered event. Then you fly in the face of all that is good and moral by cavorting with a young man. This is the last straw. You are out, missy. *Out.*"

You are too stunned to move. All these months of hard work curtseying and applying cosmetics and cutting out carbs for nothing! Before you can launch into a tirade, you feel yourself being lifted, as you are swept off your feet and cradled in Tommy's arms.

"What are you doing?" you ask.

"Rescuing you. Let's get out of here." He grins and walks toward the stage door.

Okay, so you may have been kicked out of the Miss Liberty Pageant, and lost your shot at all that prize money, and lost your chance to tell all those bitches you hated in high school to kiss your beauty queen ass. But who else can say they got the boot from the pageant for "fraternizing" with a rock star?

"You know," you whisper in Tommy's ear as you exit the theater, "I don't think I had a chance to really truly 'fraternize' with you yet."

He kisses you on the mouth, long and deep.

"You can fraternize with me all night long."

The End

There is no way you are going to get into a huddle of women clawing at a rock star. It's safer to wear a porterhouse necklace in a lion's den.

Tommy is now surrounded by six Southern states, and Miss Tennessee is gripping his arm for dear life. As Tennessee weeps and hops up and down for joy, another girl snaps a photo. Once again, Tommy throws you a pleading look, and you helplessly shrug. Fanny Mae is asking you if you understand what she has been saying and you nod, answering, "Oh yes. Thanks Fanny Mae. I will really take that to heart. Thanks for your concern." Fanny Mae looks satisfied and marches off.

You glance over at Tommy, who is now being confronted by Miss District of Columbia. "Didn't I meet you once at this gig in Washington? You're Jason's cousin, right?"

Tommy looks at Miss D.C. in confusion and says, "Uh, I have a cousin Jason, but I don't really remember meeting you . . ."

"We were near this pool table," she continues desperately, "I was wearing a purple shirt," she rambles on. You smack your forehead in embarrassment for this poor, desperate girl. Tommy's new Southern girlfriends are not as sympathetic.

"Why don't you move along, D.C.?" sneers Miss Georgia. "Why don't you stop trying to be such a little star fucker and go find yourself a *real state*?" The room suddenly goes silent. That was the ultimate insult.

"Hey, Georgia," yells Miss New York, who is now making her way over to defend D.C., "at least she's not from a slave-owning trailer park state!"

The room gasps.

"You little Yankee!" screeches South Carolina. "It's wanna-be-intellectual anti-Southern bitches like you that have killed human decency! And your state is a stinky concrete piece of shit!"

"Go home and pick some cotton!" shrieks New Jersey.

"Oh, like I'm going to take shit from some trash from a mafia state!" screams North Carolina.

Two crowds have squared off against each other, nose job to nose job. On one side, New York, New Jersey, Massachusetts, Pennsylvania, D.C., and Rhode Island stare down the Southern states of Georgia, North and South Carolina, Tennessee, and Alabama. There is no doubt that a fist fight is about to happen. You look around desperately for Fanny Mae, Tommy (who seems to have bolted), a burly stagehand, anyone who may be able to curb the imminent violence.

Then it happens.

"We kicked your Southern ass in the war," New York taunts.

Boom! Miss Georgia decks New York in the face and sends her reeling to the ground, sequins and all. Miss New Jersey uses her dragonlike fingernails to rip the bodice of South Carolina's dress. Tennessee grabs a bottle of aerosol hairspray and uses it like mace, spraying it into D.C.'s eyes. There is a tangle of sequined bodies and claws are flying, and all of the girls are shrieking like banshees. Beads pop off dresses, whizzing through the air like bullets. A fog of hairspray hovers like smoke over a battlefield. Stiletto heels are used like bayonets. Bodies hit the ground. There is no way you are getting in the middle of this fray. This time, Vermont's staying out of the Civil War.

The End